Fault Zone:

Transform

An Anthology
by the
San Francisco/Peninsula Writers Club
© 2016

Fault Zone: Transform is the sixth anthology of short stories and poems produced by the San Francisco/Peninsula Writers Club.

SHRP
Sand Hill Review Press

TABLE OF CONTENTS

Introduction

Once again the warm hearts and wild minds of the San Francisco Peninsula Branch of the California Writers Club have poured their genius, talent, and perceptions into the fault zone that is our existence here in California. This year's theme, transform, suggests change. But change for the better or for the worse? After all, transformation is not always pretty and we may not like what we are becoming. But we will, without a doubt, be changed.

Open this book and see new worlds being created, old ones destroyed, familiar worlds being warped into something unimaginable, but here imagined. See how we ourselves transform through our dreams, through our defeats and losses, any yes, through our triumphs.

It is appropriate that in this our fiftieth year, the CWC/San Francisco/Peninsula Writers Club itself is being transformed. New leadership is working to expand our vision and our reach; working from our warm new venue to extend a (metaphysical) hand to the writing community–as well as those wanting to write–focusing on growing the club, recognizing, supporting, and rewarding our accomplishments, and educating us not only in craft but in the new reality that is writing and publishing.

Any enterprise like an anthology is a collaboration. My heartfelt thanks go out to the wonderful people who helped shape this work. First, of course, the writers without whom this would not be possible. Thank you. To Tory Hartmann, past president, whose vision made the original Fault Zone: Words from the

Edge a reality. To Lisa Meltzer Penn, our first and fearless editor, Audrey Kalman who followed, and stayed on to shepherd this addition as well. To my poetry editors, Diane Moomey and again, Lisa. Fiction editors, Audrey and Linda Okerlund. Essay/memoir editor, Jeannine Gerkman. Proof readers, and copy editors, Laurel Anne Hill and Elise Frances Miller. You all saved my bacon so many times.

Ann Foster
Editor

Creating the Worlds

By Diane Lee Moomey

In the first world, the sun
rose only every other day and the moon
fell from the sky because
the gravity module worked
in theory only. Tenants refused
to move in, and the first world
was compost.

The next was an improvement although
the second-generation gravity module
slipped a disc, and everything fell sideways.
The tenants complained because
whatever they dropped the neighbors got,
and drapes were all soaked through,
though it *was* written in their lease
to keep windows shut during stormy
weather—not so much to ask.
They moved out, and the second world
was toast.

The third was nearly perfect until
the icemaker jammed and froze
the planet solid at both poles
halfway to the equator. Most of the tenants
moved out in protest, still owing rent.

It would have been a crime
to jettison a world so nearly perfect
so the Powers agreed to thaw it out
and try again. Tenants returned but this lot
smoked and fought over everything
including the thermostat—
the icemaker couldn't keep up.
All the carpeting had to be re-created,
and they moved out anyhow.

The fourth world will be non-smoking.
Would-be tenants are picketing, but everyone knows
this is the only world in town. This time around
the Powers agree to keep the red and the blue
on separate continents, and to confiscate that
internal combustion engine they are all so fond of.

The fifth world is still on the storyboard.

Fault Zone:
Transform

Ann Foster, Editor

Love Doctor

By Diane Jacobson

With one hand Claudia stroked the smooth wooden trim on her steering wheel as she cruised through the clear California night. With the other she massaged the corner of her jaw trying to knead out the nervy ache that grew from a day of clenched teeth.

She put both hands on the wheel as she approached a small silver car puttering along just below the speed limit in the center lane. She pursed her lips, shook her head, and pressed the gas pedal, unleashing more horsepower from her BMW's V8 engine.

Traffic on Highway 101 flowed heavier than she expected given that she had nursed a cup of tea for an hour after her last patient. As she sipped, she reviewed her notes from the day, growing ever more annoyed at the lack of practicality and self awareness that plagued the young tech workers, bored stay at home parents, and egotistical venture capitalists that crossed the threshold of her psychology practice. Week in week out she hoped to actually help someone who needed, no *deserved*, help, instead of just listening to the same old yammering about competitive work environments, kitchen remodels that were outdated before they were completed, and unfair Wall Street assessments.

So the heavy traffic didn't bother her. She needed an outlet for the tension that built up inside her throughout the day. She enjoyed putting her powerful car's abilities to the test, weaving past practical Japanese compacts and cars tricked out to drive and look like drag racers. As she settled into the fast lane, blowing past a crotch rocket motorcycle and powerful electric sedan, she tuned into an AM talk radio call-in show where a celebrity therapist, "Dr. Rodney," doled out ill-advised advice to hopeful callers.

"Hello Maryann, Dr. Hot Rod Rodney here, what's troubling you?" Dr. Rodney's velvety voice filled her car.

"Oh God, I'm really talking to you? To THE Dr. Hot Rod," gushed Maryann.

"Oh *mein gott!*" Claudia down shifted and pressed the gas pedal, causing the rear end of the car to swish as she whipped past an SUV.

"Yes Maryann, it is I. Tell me your trouble," came the voice of Dr. Hot Rod himself.

"Oh God. I love you," Maryann chirped.

"Thank you, I love all my fans. Now, talk to me."

"It's so embarrassing."

"Tell me, Maryann. I'm a doctor. Dr. Rodney is here for you."

Claudia could hear Maryann sniveling and breathing as if she were sitting in the passenger seat.

"It's okay. It's okay. I will help you," Dr. Rodney cooed. "Forget that thousands of people are listening. Forget them and just think of me. Close your eyes and imagine I am there with you. Now, tell me."

"Oh Dr. Hot Rod, I'm soooooo depressed. My best friend is getting married next week and the dress she is making us bridesmaids wear is soooooo ugly. It makes me look soooooo fat. Should I tell her so she won't be embarrassed when she sees how awful it is in the pictures?"

"You sound like a woman who knows how to look beautiful," Dr. Rodney replied smoothly.

"Oh, I am. I do." Maryann giggled. "Even Steve thinks the dress doesn't work on me."

"Steve?" Dr. Rodney asked.

"Steve, the groom."

Claudia had plenty of experience with people whose greatest concerns were adolescent, superficial, and short term. She had a good guess why Steve's fiancé had put Maryann in an ugly dress. This bride was no dummy. Claudia was quite certain that the poor girl was a victim of betrayal by both friend and fiancé. The marriage was doomed from the onset. Divorce within a year, Claudia predicted.

"Yes. You must tell your friend about the dress." Dr. Rodney's advice to the vapid Maryann came clearly through the airwaves but did not sit well in Claudia's agitated mind. "Just imagine if you were the bride. You would want to be told wouldn't you?"

"Oh God yes. You are so right. Of course I would," Maryann gushed.

"Please hold on Maryann, we must have a word from our sponsors. All you listeners out there, stay tuned. When we come back, we'll give Maryann a chance to call the bride, her best friend, on the air. Remember, I'm here for you. Call at 1-800-1HOTROD to talk. That's 1-800-146-8763."

Claudia's right pointer finger punched a button on the underside of her steering wheel thereby activating the voice recognition media system in the car. "Call one eight hundred one four six eight seven six three," she enunciated.

"Calling one eight hundred one four six eight seven six three. Is this correct?" Replied an electronic female voice.

"Yes."

It only took a moment for the digital data to travel from the warm cocoon of the car, to a satellite floating dutifully above the Earth, and finally to a switchboard in a suburban Atlanta office park. This switchboard was operated by what had to have been a twenty-something intern. Claudia could hear the large wad of gum in her mouth as they spoke and assumed she wore something inappropriate for a workplace. A bright pink micro mini and the Victoria Secret's version of a work blouse perhaps.

"I'd like to speak to Rodney," Claudia said.

The intern launched into her script, "Tell me, what would you like to discuss with the doctor?"

"What I would like to discuss with the 'doctor'," Claudia replied, "is none of your concern. Put me through to him."

"I'm sorry, ma'am," the intern said through her gum smacking. "Before I put you through, I have to ask you some questions."

"No thank you. But do know that I am calling to stop your boss from giving some very poor advice. Please transfer me."

Claudia could hear the sound of a posture adjustment on the other end of the phone. "I don't know if I should."

"Do it." Claudia pointed a finger stiffly at the car's media console.

"Um ..."

"Do it!" Claudia snapped with the desired effect. She was suddenly on hold listening to "a word from our sponsor", a suppository administered weight loss program that had, until recently, been a closely held secret of many perpetually thin French women.

"Welcome back! We have Maryann on the line. In a few moments she is going to tell her best friend how ugly the bridesmaid dresses in her wedding are. Keep listening it is all going to happen on the air. But first we have a caller. Who do we have Dakota?" Dr. Rodney said.

The gum chewing intern's voice came on the air, "Gosh Hot Rod, she didn't say."

"Didn't say huh?" Hot Rod's irritation was clear.

"Nope," chomped Dakota.

"And why is she calling?" Hot Rod asked.

"Gosh, she didn't say that either."

Claudia waited on hold listening to the disgruntled radio host try to pull information from the clueless Dakota. Ultimately he made the rash, unfortunate decision to gamble and take the call.

"This is Dr. Hot Rod Rodney, caller, you are on the air. What is your name?"

"Dr. Claudia Becker, Psychologist."

"Hi Claudia."

"I prefer Dr. Becker."

"Oh *do* you?" Rodney replied.

"I do."

"Why are you calling today, *Dr. Becker*?" Her name came out of his mouth as a taunt. Had he any luck or forethought, Rodney would have cut the call short. But, despite his profession, he was a poor judge of character and had little ability to sense mood or emotion in a voice.

Dakota, on the other hand, had spent a few more minutes with Claudia than her boss and seemed to have realized that he was in over his head. Frantic finger snaps and loud whispered "hang ups" and "go to commercials" echoed across the airwaves followed by the muffled sound of a door shutting.

Claudia ignored the scuffle and forged ahead. "Maryann, are you there?"

"Yep," Maryann gamely piped up.

"Maryann, you must not listen to this quack."

"Huh?"

"If you have a shred of dignity and human decency left in you, you will do as I say."

"Now wait a minute!" Rodney's incensed voice piped in.

"No, I will not. Rodney, I'm not sure how you ended up where you are but I am certain that you possess neither the skills nor education to advise anyone on dresses let alone premarital affairs. Rodney, remain in your chair and do not interrupt again as I speak to Maryann. Got it?" She continued on without pausing for Rodney's response. "Maryann, I am now speaking to you. You are in a sexual relationship with this groom, Steve, yes?"

"What! No I'm not!" Maryann protested.

"Maryann. It's time to stop lying. Believe me, facing up to this mess is the right thing to do. If you won't listen to me, then listen—I can't believe I'm actually going to say this—to Rodney. Imagine how you would feel if you were the bride. She is about to enter a marriage with a philandering man. She needs to know that her fiancé is having sex with another woman."

"I guess."

"You guess? Would you want to go forward in a commitment with someone who was unfaithful at such a time? A lifelong commitment?"

"Um, no?"

"Of course, no. Now, answer me. What is your relationship to this Steve?"

"We're together." Maryann sobbed.

"Sexually?"

"Yes. Sexually. All the time. I'm so sorry Felicia. It wasn't my fault. I didn't mean to."

Claudia interrupted. "Maryann, did someone force you?"

"No," Maryann whispered.

"Of course not. You made this choice and now you must own up to it."

"But ..."

Claudia cut her off. "Do not make excuses. Maybe someday this Felicia will forgive you. Maybe she won't. Face it. Live with it. Learn from it."

"Oh God Felicia. Please, please don't be mad at me ..." Maryann stammered and sobbed.

"Good first step Maryann. Felicia, if you are listening, I advise you to save yourself a lot of heartache and money and leave this man before you are legally tied to him." Claudia sighed. "Now, a word of advice to you Dakota, if you have your sights set on a career in broadcasting, spit out your gum and seek other employment. You have nothing to learn and everything to lose by associating with Mr. Rodney here. Good evening." With this she disconnected with the press of a button, glad to have been of some help. The tension of the day was gone.

The Man Who Adopted a Verb

By Darlene Frank

I feel round this morning, shaped like an egg, still warm from my dream, still under the bedclothes. The egg encases me in a swirling energy, comforting, as though I am merged with another—maybe God, a soulmate, my space-child self, or a birth cocoon of nebulae.

I dreamed of a man who adopted a verb in the form of a child. He seemed not to know quite what to do with it, and my girlfriend and I took him under our wing as though he himself were the child, our small gestures offering, explaining, helping. He was a gay man who lived alone, and why he wanted a child he never told us. He never said the child was a verb, nor did we, but we all understood this, without words.

The man lived a few blocks away. Our phone would ring; it would be him, asking a question about what to eat, where to go, how to get there—simple things that he seemed helpless and awkward at handling. Everywhere he went he carried the child, who as yet had no voice except to make small eating and crying sounds. The child was tender like a new green leaf, and thinking about the child nearly makes me cry.

He was devoted to the child, a boy, and kept it with him at all times. The child was an action verb, always moving from place to place in the man's arms or the baby carriage. The child was strong and alert and healthy, the son of a complete sentence.

I visited the man and sat in his living room looking at the paintings on his wall: a black Jesus and a bright blue Matisse. He was on the phone, ordering pizza in a deep Southern drawl that made him sound confident, playful, secure, and quite unlike the man I saw taking care of the child.

When we went out, we had to tell him where to sit in the car—not in the space under the hatchback, but on the back seat where he would have more room. One day I pushed the baby carriage up a long, steep hill on a city street so he could take the bus alone.

One night the phone rang. My girlfriend picked it up, listened briefly, then hung up. "It was him, saying thank you," she said. He had spoken only those two words. It was all he knew how to say at that moment.

I feel sad thinking about him, because he has only the child to keep him company, in the same way I was comforted by the warm, swirling egg around me this morning. But this is all the comfort there is, when one lies alone in bed, and this must be enough. On some mornings this is all we can feel. And we climb out of bed and walk through the day, remembering with each person we look at or speak to, that perhaps they too woke with the same feeling and are carrying it through their day. And we remember to smile and think or say a kind word, because this is what we can offer each other. For we have all adopted a verb, and are trying to raise it, awkward and questioning, getting help from whoever will give it.

Breaking Silence with Nicky-Mouse

By Martha Clark Scala

I get paid to talk. I also get paid to listen. A retreat atop a mountain at a monastery on the Big Sur coast of California held so much appeal. As this was not my first time on retreat at this location, I knew we would be asked to observe silence at all times except when we met for five ninety-minute writing sessions scattered throughout the three-day weekend. I did not hesitate; it did not even matter to me what the particular theme of the retreat would be. I just looked forward to the wonderful excuse to be in a beautiful place with no obligation to interact. My expectations were dashed thanks to an unexpected intruder.

It was one of the warmest nights I have ever spent on silent retreat at the monastery. I laid on top of my sheets with the fan pointed right at me while I read an engrossing novel. I had already swatted away a moth or two, seen a spider consider entry inside my pillowcase, and freaked out because I felt a bug make an exploratory landing at the base of the V in my V-neck t-shirt. It occurred to me I might need to sleep with bug spray slathered all over me. Ewww.

But then, something furry darted across my bare ankle.

"What the fuck was THAT?" I exclaimed out loud as I sprang from the bed.

Nothing. I saw nothing as I realized that my profane burst of sound was probably loud enough for my neighbor to hear. I wanted to go and explain to her, "Listen, I NEVER break silence here; this was an aberration!" It took a while for the startle response to quiet down but eventually I talked myself into turning off the lights and trying to get some sleep.

We had been warned that critter noises outside were normal so the first time I heard some rustling, I thought it was up on my roof as this had happened many times before. But there was a crinkle, crinkle, crinkle to this sound. "Is there a critter *inside* this time? Is it checking out my trash?" I asked myself, in silence. I am diligent about storing my garbage in a plastic bag in the fridge so I reassured myself that if nothing tasty were found in the trash can, the critter would move on.

I was wrong. Drifting off to sleep, I heard a skitter, skitter, skitter. Rustle, rustle, rustle. Crinkle, crinkle, crinkle.

Quickly, I grabbed my flashlight and pointed it at the kitchen counter not even three feet from my head. A tiny mouse, looked up to see the light, but kept right on poking around the well-contained food sitting on my counter.

Did he speak? you might ask. No, no eeks or squeaks or peeps. Just a brazen, hungry mouse.

"Get the hell out of here," I half-yelled, and half-whispered. It scampered off to the end of the counter, and out of sight, while I took all that well-contained food and put it inside my cooler.

"There," I said to myself, "now there's nothing for him to explore so that will be that."

Wrong! The flashlight caught him exploring the top of my cooler. This time, I rose from my bed to shoo the silly guy away but instead of running down the counter, he scurried right into the toaster. The nerve!

"Aha," I thought, "I will just cover the toaster, and take it outside." So I grabbed a plate, put it over the top of the toaster, and slid a tray underneath it so I could carry my temporary trap with greater ease. I was so damn smug. "How resourceful am I?" I thought.

I put the tray down on a picnic table, and just before going back inside, took the plate off to free the little guy.

"Okay, NOW, I can get some sleep," I reassured myself. But I was wrong, again.

Either the mouse got out of the toaster in the time it took me to fetch that plate, or he just knew how to get back inside. We had our last encounter of the evening about a half hour later.

The skitter, skitter, skitter started up again. I pointed the flashlight at him, again, and this time, he really paused to look right back at me with his bulging eyes, and I burst out laughing. I remain amazed that I was more amused than pissed or frightened. I really was not scared of this guy but I knew there was no way I could get any sleep if I stayed in my bed. I also draw the line at furry animals, other than my own two cats, making me their jungle gym.

I decided to sleep in my car. Eventually, I caught a few winks. But before I got comfortable, I realized that sleeping in the back seat of my car forced me to be in a fetal position. "What on earth is being birthed, now?" I wondered, "and who is the midwife? Is my car the womb?"

My brother Nick used to wait behind doors in order to pop out and scare the heck out of me with a big, loud "boo!" I would scream; he would laugh. Without fail. My startle response is off the charts. I decided to name my visiting rodent, Nicky-Mouse. I have had two different psychics tell me that my brother hovers nearby, always wanting to help.

I thanked Nicky-Mouse for bringing laughter to the middle of my night. If anyone could get me to break silence, it would be him. I told him he could have what crumbs he could find on the meticulously sponged counter, but he could not just have my food, or disturb my sleep.

I had to break silence a lot the next day—to report the issue and ask if there was any other bed on the premises, to tell the guy who came to deal with the problem that I did not think trapping the mouse or blocking its most obvious entry point would solve the problem because I was convinced it had multiple access points. Nicky-Mouse was hell-bent on scouting his territory, just as my brother Nick was hell-bent on startling me. I slept one more night in my car as there were no other available beds at the monastery. I reminded myself that some people sleep in a car *every* night. Thanks to Nicky-Mouse, I talked, I listened, and it was still a mighty fine retreat. Some people die way too young, but it looks like their work as angels keeps them busy.

Summer Place

By Sam Kauffman

A song crept into my soul today riding on the summer
    wind,
Peeking into my summer place closed for many
    season—
Windows shuttered, standing on a grassy knoll,
Whitewashed in the morning melody at the water's
    edge–
Waiting–held in time–face unchanging;
Remembering now how I loved to sit
Upon the wisteria porch in wicker chairs painted white
To smell the elfin roses reaching for the trellis top
When summer heavy hangs upon the railing
While a frisky breeze
Hop skips
Across the harbor,
Leaving diamond footsteps on the waters,
To open up the wide front door,
Decorated with a flowered wreath,
Inviting welcome to my summer place,
Warmed by summer's enduring caress,
The wide front room filled with bits of yellowed lace,
A fragile nautilus,
Daphne pressed between old diary pages,
Haunting songs of summers past,
Antique keys among the faded photographs;
Taking the album in my hands, sitting on the fragrant
    porch–

Arms around my knees, tabby kitten by my side—
To watch the games and songs
And friends
Unfold their images across the lawn—
Children playing in the sand at the water's edge,
Voices lifted in the sunlight.

Here, I touch their hands again,
Look into their eyes,
See our laughter fill the afternoon
When we return from play
Young women,
Dressed in cool white linen,
Sun touched hair bound in flowing ribbons,
Enfolded in the breezy twilight on the porch,
To feast on summer peaches
Gazing across the water
With eyes enchanted by the gathering lights
Twinkling in the dusk—
The first bright stars of evening rising on the darkened
        air,
Whispering of the future borning,
Blessed by the crickets chirping serenade
Till I stand, alone,
Upon the empty porch tightly holding in my arms
Roses—red and white,
Pink and lavender,
Yellow, crimson, orange and ivory and blue—
Their new perfume ever filling
The quiet rooms of my summer place—
Until the golden moon slowly closes the white front
        door,

Leading me upon the sandy path
To morning
Painting blush upon the sky,
Putting the key into its place
When the summer wind
Whispers
Of a summer place.

Podunk, IL

By Nanci Lee Woody

My brother, long-since dead, was barely a teenager when I, *Surprise!,* came along. He started drinking right after and never quit.

We lived in Podunk, Illinois, our shack-of-a-house dwarfed by cornfields in every direction. When my mother met my dad, she had been a widow for ten years, her young husband having died of blood poisoning before antibiotics, leaving her with a three-year old boy, an eighth grade education, and meager welfare checks.

My father, not my brother's father who was dead, was, as they say, an old-fashioned rolling stone, married with kids when he courted my lovely, lonely mother, though he never mentioned the fact to her. Some months into their courtship and without a mention to anyone who might have cared, Daddy prepared to divorce his current wife and leave for California with yet another woman.

Mother was six months along when Daddy stopped by on his way out West, and something broke inside her when he said, "Damnit, woman. I didn't promise you nothing. I'm offering you some money, here. Take it." Mother could see his about-to-be-new-wife waiting in the car.

Her throat tight, tears nearly choking her, she slapped the money out of his hand, letting pride get in the way of good sense. If Mother had known she'd soon need the money regularly for bail for my brother, who was now 13 and about to turn bad, she might have taken it. My father, figuring, I guess, that he did his duty when he tried to help his unborn child, disappeared, driving west never to be seen again by mother, never to be seen at all by me.

This was the 40s, not a time when bastard children were held up in front of the congregation, blessed and brought gifts. This was a time when, if you were unmarried, it was shameful to get pregnant. People acted like you were contagious, saw you coming down the sidewalk and they'd cross the street to avoid having to say something to you. Thus my mother never left her tiny house once she started to show, but everybody knew anyway. Podunk being the town it was, telephone party lines were always buzzing. People hung out on their front porches in their rockers pretending to listen to the radio, watching what everybody else was doing.

On the evening of my birth, mother had waited, knowing, by the front window for over an hour, one hand holding her belly, the other making a little hole in the lace curtain to see out, watching the flaming oranges, reds and yellows float to the ground, pile up. When I started my exit to the outside world, she let the contractions come as she stood there, bending slightly, never crying out. No sooner had my brother left his 8th grade classroom and walked home than her water broke. She was embarrassed, having that happen in front of Donny, and he was mortified, having to witness it. She motioned for him to come to her, help her to bed. She asked him to bring some towels, a chamber pot and her nightgown. Then, "Please," she said, "just leave me alone now. I'll call when I need you."

For the next few hours, she suffered the pains of childbirth alone. At some point between contractions, she called for Donny, told him to go next door and ask to borrow their phone so he could call the doctor. Donny hesitated, as he always disliked advertising their poverty in this way. Dejected, he left her bedside, went outside, sloshed his feet through the leaves, rapped on the neighbor's door, said he was sorry it was so late, but his mother was sick and could he please use their phone?

The neighbors stood nearby as Donny was talking to the doctor who'd had a long day and was grumpy, yet knew well his mother's situation. "Can't it wait 'til morning, Son?"

Donny wanted to scream and run out of that house, but he held tightly to his composure as he told the doctor his mother needed him bad so please please please come right away. He hung up the phone before the doctor could ask anything else and ignored the neighbors' offers to help-in-any-way-they-could as he ran for the front door.

Donny let the doctor in, pointed to the open bedroom door, waited in the next room until the doctor called his name. "I need some help here, Son. Come on in now." The doctor was fussing with the sheets, wet, bloody. When they rolled his mother over, pulled the dirty sheets away, she cried out. Donny's gut seized, his heart pounded, tears rolled from his eyes. "Get some clean sheets, now. Hurry on," he was told.

Donny couldn't find clean sheets because his mother owned only the set that was on her bed. He didn't know what to do. He found a clean towel and brought that to the doctor.

As Donny brought in the towel, the doctor grabbed my head, pulled, and finally, there I was, oxygen deprived and blue as the early morning sky. He wrapped me in the towel and laid me in my mother's arms.

"Well, now. We've got us a girl. Do we have a name for her?"

My mother, exhausted, shook her head "no."

"I know you've thought about this. There's forms here to fill out. Would it be too much trouble if you told me now?"

Mother had even less money after I was born. She sent Donny to the food lines to get whatever he could and bring it home. He earned the nickname, "Soupy," which he hated and of course it stuck all through high school until he lied about his age, joined the Navy when I was four years old and left Podunk.

When he came home on leave, he would play his guitar and say, "This one's for you, little sister," and sing "Danny Boy."

But if ye come and all the flowers are dying. If I am dead, as dead I well may be, you'll come and find the place where I am lying, and kneel and say an Ave there for me.

Then the boozing would start, the demons would take hold. His newly acquired knowledge of electronics guided him as he hooked the radio to the iron to amplify the sound. He tuned in at full volume the Holy Roller preachers from Nashville. When the preacher shouted, "Hallelujah, Brother!" Donny would let loose with a chilling, demonic laugh and spit curses at Jesus Christ all throughout the miserable night, torturing our mother and me.

Donny re-enlisted as long as they'd have him, but when I was in high school, he received a medical discharge. Paranoid schizophrenic, the papers said, and he voluntarily checked himself into a mental hospital. Every month. The routine was, on the day his disability check appeared in the mail, he'd leave the psychiatrists and the hospital and the AA meetings, stock up on booze, stay at mother's house until the money ran out, then return to the hospital for a free ride until the next check arrived.

Some nights, with drawn fist he'd threaten Mother, or he'd smash what little furniture she had and toss it into the coal-burning stove, until he'd finally succumb to a booze-induced stupor on the rat-eaten couch, puke and piss his pants and soil the couch, and wake up mean. I couldn't stand being around him and was sure he felt the same way about me.

I made up my mind to quit high school, get as far away from Podunk and Donny, and mother because she put up with him, as I could. She knew what I was feeling and going through and was conflicted about what to advise me, but Donny strong-armed his way into our conversation, told me I'd better not even think about not graduating from high school. He wouldn't allow it! He raved on, the broken vessels in his nose getting redder, saying I only had one year of high school left and didn't I have good grades? Anybody could get a job as a telephone operator. Bookkeepers and waitresses were a dime a dozen. Didn't I want to make something of myself, for God's sake? Or did I want to wind up a crazy drunk like him? Then the laugh, the demon pouring out of him. He finished his tirade with threatening to make me miserable if I brought up quitting high school again.

In spite of never getting a decent night's sleep and slinking to school when his name was on the front page of the local paper (which he called *The Daily Asswipe*) for drunk and disorderly conduct, I managed to graduate. The *Podunk Daily News* published a short article about me, first kid in the family to graduate high school, get a scholarship, and go on to college, blah blah blah.

When I finished college, I, like my daddy some 20 years earlier, headed for California. I didn't think about Donny except to hold on to a fierce hatred of him. I had been teaching for two years when I got the phone call from my Mother. She was sobbing, could hardly talk, said through her tears that she had failed her son, told me Donny's body was found in Lake Michigan, unidentifiable except for his dental work. Nobody knew anything about the circumstances of his death, though likely he was murdered.

In his abandoned Studebaker were found just a few things: a six-pack with four missing Pabst Blue Ribbon beers, a wallet with ID but no money, a letter from the VA hospital inquiring as to his whereabouts, and the folded, worn newspaper article from the

Podunk Daily News with my picture and high school graduation announcement in it. In the margin, in his handwriting, were the words, "my little sister."

Learning the Bones

By Laurel Anne Hill

My friend, Carmela, owned a large box of bones—a gift from her relatives. Hadn't she said so mere moments ago? How strange. I waited for her explanation. Or even for her laugh.

Instead, she shifted position on the laboratory stool across from mine, then told me about the medical school in her home country—in the West Indies. Her hands reached into the plastic tub on the counter as she chatted. She knotted the end of a wet strip of cellulose tubing. I did the same. One of our jobs today was transforming flat, limp tubing into little bags.

"You won't believe what my family did so I could learn the bones." Carmela's ebony hair, not quite shoulder length, shifted as she tilted her head. Her eyes avoided mine. "They went to a graveyard. At night. Dug up a body. Grandma boiled stuff clean. I kept the box under my bed."

A human body? Stolen and boiled in a huge pot? This was the real-life nineteen-seventies, not a grave robber scene from a Charles Dickens' novel. She had to be kidding.

"I needed them for anatomy class." Carmela tightened a knot. "Our school didn't have such good supplies. You people in the United States take so much for granted."

Human bones. She wasn't kidding. If I'd opened my eyes any wider, my eyeballs would have fallen out and rolled on the floor. A skeleton or two lurked in the closets of most families. But Carmela had stashed a real one under her bed. Had she become a physician in her own country? She certainly wasn't a doctor here in California.

She kept knotting. I stuffed a marble into the bottom of each ready bag. A tight fit. We would use the weighted bags, as always, to purify blood samples in a buffer-filled tank—to get rid of interfering substances. Then we could test for a protein linked to certain cancers.

"I get married," Carmela said, "but I still want to be a doctor. When my husband slept, I lifted the box onto my side of our bed and studied the bones. Then one night he starts waking up at the wrong time. Reaches out, eyes closed, to touch me and feels something else." She shrugged, her mouth curving in a tentative smile. "That was the end of medical school for me."

Such a scene would have been hilarious in a British comedy. In real life, however, an unfulfilled educational dream was no laughing matter. How frustrating for Carmela. She must have resented her husband's attitude. The decision must have disappointed her family, too. Her grandma had boiled those bones clean for nothing.

I once had hoped to earn a Ph.D. in immunology. Due to finances and family obligations, the opportunity had never arisen. I'd achieved an M.S. in biology, though. My mother had helped me procure copies of scientific articles. My grandmother had baked bran muffins and savory casseroles to offer me strength and encouragement. She'd even boiled a chicken carcass to create fragrant and tasty broth. Thankfully, she'd discarded the bones as household trash. No macabre box lurked under my bed.

With luck, none ever would.

Twenty-five years passed. Several of my careers morphed into new ones. I went to work for a pharmaceutical research site. Yet I kept in touch with Carmela and never forgot about her learning the bones. Then, on what should have been an ordinary day, I received a phone call at work from my daughter, Alicia.

Alicia's voice sounded strained. For this conversation, I wanted privacy. I closed my office door, sat down, then planted my elbows on my desk. I braced myself for what might come next.

Alicia, in her second year of law school, expressed reservations about completing her studies. I clutched the phone receiver. My mouth wouldn't form words. I hadn't braced myself well enough.

"I've learned so much," she continued. "I really appreciate the opportunity you and Dad have given me. But I'll never work in some high-powered attorney's office. That's just not me. I feel as though I'm wasting your money."

How could she talk this way? Alicia, with a dramatic arts undergraduate degree from New York University, worked hard and passed exams in Tulane University's well-regarded law school program. No easy transition. My husband and I had dug up the money to help her succeed. Boiled away obstacles. The least she could do was bury her doubts, resurrect her enthusiasm, and finish learning the law bones.

But was I thinking this way to benefit her? Or because David and I would be disappointed? She hadn't actually said she planned to quit. Did she really want to drop out of law school at all? I listened to her voice. Somewhere, under those words lay her real distress. What would reveal it? I had to find a way to provide helpful advice.

Two years ago, acceptance to Tulane had elated Alicia. What had changed? Her father was in his seventies. Student loans and David's retirement account funded her graduate studies. She often called to discuss potential expenditures. Fear of family financial disaster might have fueled her current worries. Yet, was money her only concern?

I thought about our previous conversations. Alicia liked to bake cookies for friends and do volunteer work at animal shelters. Her internship this past summer had been with an organization protecting abused children. Ambition and avarice motivated some lawyers. Alicia was sensitive to the needs of others. Did she wrongly perceive a mismatch between her personality and the law profession? Then I remembered something she'd told me.

"No one takes me seriously," she had said.

I pictured her honey-blonde hair, long eyelashes and shapely figure. In teen theater, she'd frequently played the sexy airhead. Did some of her current peers typecast her in this same manner? Even tease her?

Another unfulfilled educational dream could be waiting to happen.

But Alicia was perceptive and intelligent. She enjoyed her law classes. Was capable of finding a niche. I brushed back a lock of my graying hair, determined to provide the best advice I could.

"You need to finish what you've started," I said, trying to sound firm, yet understanding and motherly. "There are opportunities other than typical law offices. You just have to find one right for you. And you haven't flushed our financial security—or your own— down the toilet."

During the next few months, Alicia made no more mention of quitting Tulane. I thought about her a lot. I worried. I thought about Carmela, too. Carmela and her husband had eventually separated. She ran a medical laboratory in her home country. Her daughters were doing well in school. And I was studying to take the California Underground Storage Tank Operator licensing exam, needed for my job in hazardous materials management. My books and notes sat in a bag beside my bed. Too dusty underneath. New days brought us all new bones to learn.

Alicia called me at work again. This time she reported she'd found a potential summer internship in New York, for a manager of bands and other entertainers. Her dramatic arts background would be perfect for an entertainment law career. This intern position could provide insight into the business. Some agents had law degrees, another possible choice. I crossed my fingers, toes and eyes—anything to bring good luck. I also prayed hard.

"I love my new job. My boss is fantastic," Alicia told me on the phone one afternoon, bubbling more than a washing machine overloaded with suds. "I finally know how I'm going to use all my education. Really help people. I can hardly wait to graduate. I can see myself doing this for the rest of my life."

Years ago, Carmela's family and my own had used fundamental skills to encourage us to follow our dreams. Career doors had opened, even if not the portals we'd envisioned. Many routes could lead toward rewarding lives.

Education provided the supporting structure—the skeleton—to stretch and grasp future opportunities. But who people were and what values they treasured breathed life into the dry bones of learning, and, ultimately, into themselves. Achieving real success meant struggling and learning to unearth inner strength. It meant discovering when to boil off obstacles and how to dialyze away what interfered with seeing truth.

Achieving real success also meant lighting the lamps to guide younger generations. A bone worth remembering. I smiled.

Exercise

By Jeannine Gerkman

I don't want to exercise
If only I was a sloth
I could find a branch and rest there
Or cocoon like a moth

Why can't I just hibernate
Like a bear in his cave?
I don't want to face outside
Be courageous, firm and brave

I want to be like an oyster
Snug within my shell
Like deep dark murky water
I want to sit for a spell

I don't want to leap for a jumping jack
Bend and touch my toes
No I don't want to stretch my back
Why you do, heaven knows

Yes my limbs are a bit flabby
And my tummy pooches so
You're right I'm somewhat crabby
But I want you to know…

FAULT ZONE: Transform

That I don't like getting sweaty
To grunt and pant and groan
Why can't you just 'get' me
And leave well enough alone?

So don't hand me a ball, mitt or bat
Don't meet me at the track, or sit me on a mat
Rather, set me loose along a meadow, hillock or glen
Put me in the middle of nature, I'll be happy then

I want to tramp in the forest
Breathe in the rich scent of pine
Feel the bark with my fingertips
You've got your bliss, I've got mine

I want to hunker down in tide pools
With water to my knees
Have a conversation with starfish
I'd like that, if you please

Look for lizards on the sidewalk
And ants up in a line
Hawks on the highest treetops
Uh huh, that'd be just fine

I want to hold my breath in wonder
When a hummingbird flies my way
I want to listen to the thunder
And sleep my nights away

I really don't like to exercise

But I love to explore and see
I want beauty and the unexpected
Won't you come along with me?

Pearls

By Diane Lee Moomey

Pearl Divers, who dare to go deep, who bring up treasure; divers who know the breathing, the singing, whistling breathing that pushes oxygen deep into the cells—women who tie back their long hair, who disappear for whole minutes, then with hands full break the surface in the nimbus of their own air bubbles.

"You have to be wholesome," the Ama tells the camera. "You can't be stressed or worried when you dive."

She fastens the snaps of the wetsuit, pulls up her hood, wipes the glass of the facemask clean and fits it over her nose and eyes. This camera and this Ama, this Diving Woman, are in Japan, seaside, at Shirahama. A group of eight village women talks the diving Life. They are bold, outspoken, in a manner not usually associated with Japanese women of a certain age.

The rope around the waist, tied to the wooden bucket: the cold! the risk! Of drowning, of sharks . . . the bravery! Perhaps rapture of the deep, though these women do not go very far down. Bravery—at every moment a finger's-breadth from the Edge, nudging that edge in such a gentle way, a knowing way. Staying in Now, because Now is the only place to be.

The risk! The giant's hand that grips your spine when the air is gone!

"We know our limits and we don't go beyond them," this Ama, Michiko, continues earnestly. "We take only what we can see. The men, they'll turn over big rocks and ruin the nesting sites. That's the men. We women are careful not to do that, not to take too many, to make sure there are enough for next year and the year after. We have our rules, and we keep them.

"It's hard! You see those abalone and you think, 'I want them all!' and you go after just one more, and stay down too long. Once I had that feeling in my back, the terrible feeling and I knew I was out of air, I might not make it back up.

"One woman drowned right over there, a while ago. She stayed down too long, she drowned."

What you have in common, my sisters, my amas, my poets, is that you are all pearl divers: intrepid, pushing water aside until you reach the oyster bed, staying in the depths, coaxing the stubborn shells from their hiding places, pushing these shells open, carrying the pearl to the surface where you will whistle and gasp for breath again.

Not only pearls. Not even many pearls. Mostly—we must be truthful—abalone and seaweed, other good food. Useful, sensible things.

But once in every hundred dives, a true pearl . . . .

If you are lucky, my poets, you will have time to put on your wetsuit when the call comes. Time to snap the snaps that secure the torso covering over the leggings, wipe down your goggles, adjust your hood. Time to tie the weights around your waist, then one end of the rope on top of that, the other end to the bucket.

Then you'll slip over the side of the boat. This is a choice, after all. You'll float a moment upon the surface, filling your cells with good air. If you are lucky, you know exactly what it is you are diving for, and where it is. You may even be able to see it from the boat.

They call themselves old, these women: they are seventy, eighty—one is ninety. They plan to dive as long as they can. The tanned, smooth skin! strong! The stride! They worry that theirs may be the last generation—few young women want to do this work.

"I started diving when I finished high school. It was the only work for a woman in those days! We wore the white shorts, then, with white shirt and headscarf with lucky signs printed on it. Sharks don't like white.

"We didn't have masks then, but the water was clearer. We could see. It was so cold two meters from the bottom! Not like now—it's warmer now—but then it was so cold! We'd come back out after a dive and run to the fire in the Ama hut to get warm!"

But sometimes the call comes suddenly. You may find yourself briefly clad and shivering, pushing yourself to the bottom against your own buoyancy, water filling your eyes. You turn small rocks gently, fill your hands, hurry back to the boat where your man may be waiting, blowing out all the while. When you reach the surface the final blast of air left in your lungs escapes "wheeeeeee" in a long whistle, a gasp of new air, a whistle again.

"When I first started diving, we wore just a loincloth." This Ama is one of the oldest, in her eighties. "We had nothing on top! It was hard. They looked down on us you know: with our beliefs, it's low-class to expose your body. But somebody needed to do it, and we didn't care!"

You may be nearly naked, swimming out far to a place you know already. Your sisters may be, may not be with you but you go regardless because you have made your choice. You could plead faintness or simply collapse upon the beach—who would make you dive if you are lying limp on the sand?—but you go. You know what you are looking for. You know you are a tempting morsel for sharks but you go; it must be done.

Or this, my poets, my painters: it may be already night when you are awakened, alone and in water over your head, completely naked and unprepared. You could try to swim to shore. Or you could stay—you have heard that treasure exists in these waters and can be found by touch alone. You decide to dive because you seek that pearl, the one precious thing: the perfect sentence, the perfect color, the perfect form, the melody so sublime that listeners swoon on hearing it, the answer to the one question you have been asking your entire life. You dive and dive until you find that. You dive and hope to gain the beach again when you are ready to leave the water.

If you are lucky, you will like this diving; after the dozenth time you will have developed a taste for it as you might for urchin or for squid. You will seek it, again and again will plunge and fill your bucket, bring it home

You may be nearly naked, swimming out far to a place you know already. Your sisters may be, may not be with you but you go regardless because you have made your choice. You could plead faintness or simply collapse upon the beach—who would make you dive if you are lying limp on the sand?—but you go. You know what you are looking for. You know you are a tempting morsel for sharks but you go; it must be done.

Or this, my poets, my painters: it may be already night when you are awakened, alone and in water over your head, completely naked and unprepared. You could try to swim to shore. Or you could stay— you have heard that treasure exists in these waters and can be found by touch alone. You decide to dive because you seek that pearl, the one precious thing: the perfect sentence, the perfect color, the perfect form, the melody so sublime that listeners swoon on hearing it, the answer to the one question you have been asking your entire life. You dive and dive until you find that. You dive and hope to gain the beach again when you are ready to leave the water.

"We're well past our expiration date!" laughs one. "We just keep going!" The other Amas nod in agreement.

"You have to like diving or you just can't do it."

If you are luckiest of all, you will have companions: sister-divers who take the plunge with you, who know all about the gasping whistle, the gripping in the spine, the dark shape that might be sharks; the white shirt with scarf and pants that keeps those sharks at bay. Sisters who know all about, and will marvel at, the treasure you finally bring up.

"Aaaaaahhhhh," they will intone, as you will do for them, "how magnificent!" and you will sit around your fire and marvel at the lives you lead.

Taut
they move across the heights
spinning phases of a moon
never full
quiet as clouds
above the tall pines
hawk

By Bill Baynes

The Drive

By Belinda Chua

A month before she died from lung cancer at 52, my best friend, Sunny, asked me to take her for a drive. Emaciated and grey, she curled up in the passenger seat beside me. We cruised along an oak-canopied two-lane back road, the sun's setting rays dappling the windshield. Quietly she observed my hands turning the steering wheel. Then she sighed and looked away. Her middle finger traced a pattern into the condensation on the window. "So many things I can't do anymore," she rasped.

"Aw, Sunny, you've lived your life fast and furious. You've done more than most people I know," I said. "Compared to me..."

"Compared to you," she jumped in, her voice suddenly strong, "I've done three times as much as you have."

Her habit of finishing my sentences never failed to grate on my nerves. She straightened up. "Three times." She waved three fingers next to my face, the corner of her eyes crinkling.

I flinched. "Right." Then I backed down. "Meaning, if I'm fifty years old," I calculated, "you've done the equivalent of a hundred and fifty years of stuff?" I turned to her. "That's a heck of a lot of stuff."

Her chuckle ended in a fit of racking cough that rustled her now over-sized navy blue down jacket. "That's right." She swallowed. "It is a lot."

Later that evening in the shower, with the heat of pelting water on the tight muscles of my upper back, I closed my eyes. The words returned to me: three times what I had done. What did that mean? Three times my accomplishments? My attempt to reassure her of her significance came back to bite me in the form of a pissing contest. Couldn't she have said a few words of acknowledgment about me—words I could find solace in, so that when I search my memory in the days to come for tit-bits of affirmation, I could tell myself that someone who had known me well, had found me—special?

•

For the thirty odd years that we'd been friends, wherever we went, Sunny insisted on driving. She was an impatient driver, a tailgater, she got speeding tickets and DUI infractions. I was Granny behind wheels, calling, "Watchit, watchit!" When her license was suspended and the courthouse was too far for her to get to on her bike, I drove her to her court hearing. The day she got her license back, we went out for pancakes to celebrate. Over short stacks drenched in blueberry maple syrup and butter, she swore with great sincerity, "This is it. I can't get into this kind of trouble anymore." Then after she dropped me off in front of my house, I heard the gun of her metallic blue two-seater as it roared down the street. I ran back to the street in disbelief and caught sight of her hand running over the back of her gelled spiked hair. Then she was gone, off to see a new lover—a young, long-haired beauty.

I hadn't met this young woman, but it was obvious that Sunny was star struck. Maybe it was because this new lover was intoxicatingly beautiful. Or maybe it was because she was married—to a man who adored her so much that he allegedly agreed to her spending nights away from home without protest.

"What's it like to be the 'other woman'?" I'd asked Sunny.

She threw me a 'you'll-never-know' look.

"Does it bother you though—you know...?" I persisted.

"No." She answered abruptly. "I'm a free agent." She lowered her gaze. "Anyway. She says I'm hot in bed."

I felt warmth rising to my neck. I lowered my eyes.

"Imagine that," Sunny continued, a smile in her voice. "I'm a hottie."

Not too many months earlier, Sunny's live-in partner of seven years had left her. One day, she came home from work, and the partner was gone, having taken only two suitcases of clothes. She had left all her other belongings behind, and a note saying she wanted to learn to live on her own. Over the phone with me, Sunny wailed. She recognized the signs too late: her partner's unexplained moodiness and reticence that had gone on for months, the chain-smoking on the corridor outside their apartment.

But now Sunny was enamored with this long-haired beauty. Over our pancake breakfast she had pulled up the young beauty's picture on her phone. "Gorgeous," I murmured.

Before long, the young beauty returned to her husband. Sunny vowed that she'd never get into another serious relationship.

"Just you watch," she told me. She made good on this promise as she sailed through a series of short-lived romantic dalliances, each one filled with storybook drama.

Once when she told me that one girlfriend was history and she was moving onto the next, I teased her, "You're not breaking off your relationships just to prove your point, are you?"

"You wouldn't understand," she retorted, "all you do is stay home and keep to the same life."

She was referring to the fact that I was still with the same man I married over two decades ago. In our middle aged years, it wasn't hard to see that my husband and I had influenced each other in the way that long term couples do, polishing each other's rough edges, but also erasing each other's individuality and verve. No longer was I the edgy person who possessed a sense of adventure. I must have looked hurt. Because Sunny conceded sheepishly as an afterthought, non sequitur, "But you do have better grammar."

I stopped, then added, "And a bigger vocabulary."

When Sunny met her next live-in partner she announced to me, her cheeks flushed, "This is it." She emphasized, "IT-it." With this woman, Sunny found a sense of calm that had previously eluded her. They lasted a while, then later parted as friends. Toward the end of Sunny's life, it was this woman who came back to lie in bed with her at night, wrapping her arms around Sunny's cold bony body which lost warmth little by little, softly caressing Sunny's hollowed cheeks as they fell asleep together.

•

Sleeping well was one of the great gifts my friend was endowed with. According to Sunny, she had never had a sleepless night. Even when emotional turbulence bore down hard, she slept. "Like a pig," was the way she put it.

"Really?" I asked, "Do pigs sleep more soundly than any other animals? Do pigs ever get insomnia?" Sunny shrugged. But I was genuinely curious. During the time that Sunny and that last partner were together, I was going through what turned out to be four and a half years of insomnia, where I got two to three hours of sleep a night if I was lucky.

"I don't get insomnia," Sunny told me, meaning, she couldn't fathom even the idea of it.

"Nothing to get," I snapped. I circled my hand around my head. "You're ON when you want to be OFF. Like a toaster." My voice grew louder. I knew I sounded crazy. "After it's toasted enough bread, it's time to turn off, cool down." She understood that. She loved toasted sandwiches of all kinds. "I'm the toaster. I can't turn off, and I can't unplug. I keep toasting and toasting. And I feel like I'm gonna explode."

The need to blurt out the indescribable frustration was like a huge raging fever. The back of my eyes burned. I blinked furiously. I had lain in bed at all odd hours of the day, every day, praying for sleep, which rarely came. I avoided people, commitments and responsibilities. Never having been one to venture far, I was now confined to the house out of exhaustion—rendering me totally ineffectual. The shame was deep.

Sunny nodded. Quiet. And after a while, in that deep silence, the tears that I had kept dammed behind my eyes flowed out silently. Sunny held her tongue, sat unmoving, until the tears stopped and the light through the window changed.

It took a while, but eventually, rest came. My body, exhausted from those years of sleeplessness, slowly learned to drop into the soft space of oblivion when night fell.

•

Sixteen months earlier, when she'd found out her diagnosis, Sunny had called me late at night.

"This is it." she said, her voice heavy and low. "What do you think I should do?"

No words came. My right hand, which had been holding the phone, began to shake uncontrollably. I resisted the urge to hang up.

"You there?" she asked.

"Go to bed," I said finally, then after a moment, added, "and drink lots of water."

"Why?"

"Because," I told her. "It's good for everything."

A few days later, after the oncologist had confirmed the diagnosis and the visit was over, Sunny and I lingered in the doctor's exam room. We had lost all reason to rush. I stared down at the plush upholstered chair I was sitting on and traced the squiggly pattern on the ash pink cushion fabric with my index finger. Sunny said she wanted to start giving her things away. But, what if you end up living another gazillion years? I asked. She said then she'd phone up her friends and ask for all her stuff back. Like, Umm, sorry Buddy...need my stuff back...

We played out her last day with black humor and hubris. She asked if I would be at her bedside.

"You kidding me?" I tried to sound flippant. "And give up my final chance to tell you all the things you did that ticked me off all these years?"

Never one to forego a good fight, she said she'd bolt up in bed to refute everything I said.

"You do that," I pointed a finger at her. "I dare you."

We laughed.

•

Having watched her lose ground steadily over the next months, I knew on the day she asked me to take her for a drive that, the end was near. Yet, clearly recognizing that each time I saw her here on out was to be one of the last times we would be together did not entirely wipe out my indignation at her words. There under the shower that night, my shoulders tensed. She had what? Done three times as much as I had? Right. Whatever.

Not long before the end, I sat by her on her blue and white striped sofa in her TV room as she labored for breath. She handed me a brown paper lunch bag secured with masking tape. Inside was a toy koala bear, the one I had coveted for years, the one with a music box embedded in its body, still looking like new. It had sat for many years on Sunny's shelf among her collections of tchotchkes, then had retired into storage in her garage. "When you die, I want first dibs on that bear," I had told her once upon a time. Now, her voice reduced to a hush, "Surprise."

My fingers grasped the brass key that protruded from the koala's chest and turned until it wouldn't turn any more. We listened to the metallic tinkling of the simple tune, playing at too fast a tempo, then slowing with each go-around. It reminded me of baby music, the kind that comes on when a mobile turns above a crib. As the music slowed to the point where it started to go out of tune, I blurted out that I had been busy making plans. I was going to learn to play jazz piano, I wanted to exercise and get strong, I wanted to travel to Santa Fe, travel to the Far East, I wanted to write a book on...

"On me." Sunny finished my sentence.

I squelched the old familiar irritation. No, I shook my head. "I want to write a book on..."

"Are you doing all these things in a hurry because of...?" She pointed to herself with both hands. The question was a brisk angry rasp.

I realized then, sitting next to her with her eyes hollow, sunken deep in their sockets—she was the only person in the world with whom I could have braved that question truthfully.

"Yeah," I said. "It scares me—to run out of time."

Her gaze dropped. Then her bony hand, blotchy and bruised, reached toward me on the sofa.

"You're right," she said finally, her voice tender and uneven. "The slow poke that you are, you need to get moving."

In the end, she was too weak to move even in bed. Her eyelashes were gummed down at the corners with soft mucus. I wanted to wipe them for her, but was afraid I'd hurt her. I remembered what I'd told her I would be there to say... *Oh, and let me tell ya—you irritate the hell outta me when you finish my sentences. And listen to this, you frigging drive me crazy speeding on the freeways trying to kill us both. And, for your information...* But, my bravado failed me. My best friend was leaving, speeding ahead of me as she had always done—into unseen space where I couldn't follow.

I leaned in close. I had meant to say goodbye. But what came out instead, was "Good night," in a strained whisper. I don't know why I said that, except maybe it was because evening was the time of day she'd always said she loved best. The time of day when, even as troubles remained, she knew she was about to lay them down. Or, maybe it was my way of telling her that I will be traveling much further into the night hours ahead, further than I had ever before—three times as far. And that I'll finally be catching up with her...in the morning.

Growing Up Green

By Ollie Mae Trost Welch

WINTER

When I was a kid in the country,
where Osage Indians once ran barefoot like
me
and the one-room school house was reached
by a narrow, swaying, swinging bridge,
leading to an icy path along the cliff,

then I, at school at last, plunged
near frozen fingers into a pail
of waiting water that I might hold
a pencil in this red, red hand.

SPRING

School let out early
so farm children could help
plant the valleys green.

Endless buckets of creek water
were poured on tender tomato plants
and melons grew: round,
ripe, and ready to eat, chilled
in the hillside spring.

FAULT ZONE: Transform

SUMMER

We went wading on slippery rocks
where sycamore brush grew over the creek
forming an endless umbrella.

We picnicked in cool caves
and sometimes found an Indian arrowhead;
picked wild blackberries
whose purple goodness stained
our lips and finger tips; (some
were picked for selling, sent to town
by Mother's horse and buggy).

We gathered wild greens from the woods
to supplement our supper: dock,
dandelion, and poke, wild berries—
we were gatherers then
like the Osage before us.

AUTUMN

Ours was sugar cane country
where horses ground round-and-round
the fired-up molasses mill.

Fall was Summer's last breath:
October's glorious gifts
appeared on Nature's stage on cue

and we were carried away by color,
by Earth's great song-and-dance
when each leaf in turn takes its bow
and drifts into the well seasoned earth.

Kennedy vs. Nixon

By Kevin Arnold

The first time Art Anthony thought about politics was when he was sixteen, the year John Kennedy challenged the incumbent vice president, Richard Nixon, for President. Art described the candidates' personalities, as he saw them, to his Republican father. His father listened for a while, but closed things off by saying, "Well if you can't vote for the man, vote for the party. Formed by Lincoln, you know. Even you have to know he was a great man. If nothing else, vote against the unions. Wait until you try to get something done. They mess everything up."

He and his father wanted to see eye to eye, but they couldn't. Art thought there was something a little greasy about Richard Nixon, especially as contrasted to Jack Kennedy's style and wit; his father was rock-ribbed.

That spring the Democratic candidate visited the high school where Art was starting his junior year. The trip to his high school was either a move calculated to gather votes in a Republican stronghold, as his father described it, or a chance to reunite with one of his old PT 109 buddies, as JFK's campaign said. Staffers and police were there, but security was so lax that Art was never searched for weapons and, when Jack extemporaneously stepped into the crowd, Art got to shake JFK's hand. The handshake was quick but memorable—Jack Kennedy looked him right in the eye.

Art and his Dad couldn't watch the evening news together; one of them would leave the room and then the other. Art's father wanted his son to understand the importance of capitalism. Art's mother stayed neutral, but Art knew she was only trying to avoid tension. Art began to viscerally dislike Nixon, so he had a harder time pretending he was anywhere close to neutral. "I hear he's a good poker player," he said.

"That's better than buying votes with giveaway programs," his Dad replied.

After the first televised debate, the radio audience agreed with his father that Nixon had won, while TV viewers and Art felt it was Kennedy's victory; that Nixon, his makeup running under those strong lights, looked scared.

What followed was the closest election up until then in the modern era, a margin of .01 percent. Although the NY Times called it for Kennedy the day of the election, it seemed for a while that they might have spoken too soon. The Anthony family, along with everyone else, was as transfixed by waiting for the final results as it had been by the campaigns. Kennedy was elected the youngest President ever, and the first non-Protestant. Art loved it when Kennedy would get on TV, his feet slowly moving his rocking chair, and speak to the country. His father thought Art was a sucker for these chats, and maybe he was, but Art, remembering how Jack had looked him in the eye, felt the man was speaking honestly.

•

Although the Kennedy vs. Nixon battle was in one sense consummated with that one election, it never really ended.

When, a thousand days into his term, Kennedy was shot, Art was working a meal job in Ann Emory Hall, a women's dorm in Madison, Wisconsin. He was washing dishes, spraying racks of silverware in the kitchen, when one of the waiters came in with a full tray of dishes on his shoulder and shouted, "The President's been shot." Soon Art sat with the waiters and women around the TV. Along with the rest of the country, they watched in disbelief as Walter Cronkite tried, unsuccessfully, to hold back the tears as he announced the death of John Fitzgerald Kennedy.

When Art called home three days after President Kennedy was shot, his father commented, "I'm waiting for them to roll away the stone."

Years later, Art was in the Mediterranean when John F. Kennedy's younger brother, Robert, then running in the Presidential race of 1968, too, was shot. "Bobby" had been tough against organized crime, which Art respected him for, perhaps even more than the smoother Jack, whom he was so proud to have met.

After he heard over the Armed Forces Radio Network that Bobby was shot, Art went into La Spezia, Italy, where his ship was anchored out, and wandered the town's back streets. Dazed, he got lost in the rabbit warren of narrow medieval streets. He was not only mourning Bobby's death but also lamenting the political implications, which Art felt meant Nixon would, after all, win the White House.

When Richard Nixon won the presidency that year, Art felt a sense of trepidation for the country. This seemed to be borne out six years later when, in order to avoid removal from office by impeachment, Nixon became the only president in American history to resign while in office. Of all the emotions that Art felt when Nixon said his final goodbyes, the strongest, and strangest, was a sadness. For Richard Nixon, of course. He was amiable in his best moments, like a guy down the street who was in over his head. But Art's sadness was also for himself and the wide gulf that now separated him from his father.

The Sad Case of the Drunken Turkish Sailor

By Kevin Arnold

Even though dock space was dear in Italy, the ship scheduler in Naples always seemed to find space for the flagship of the Sixth Fleet to tie up alongside the pier. Two smaller ships were tied up outboard of the cruiser, so their crews had to cross Art Anthony's ship to come and go. Next to the cruiser was a US Navy destroyer. Lashed outboard that ship was a smaller US Navy World War II destroyer converted to the Turkish Navy.

Ens. Anthony was standing as Officer of the Deck the evening a weaving Turkish sailor came back from liberty, his shirttail out and his jacket askew, obviously drunk. It wasn't Art's job to get involved, so he let him pass and followed him around to the other side of the ship to see how he fared. He crossed the US destroyer without incident but the officer on the Turkish ship confronted him. The sailor took a wild swing, hitting the officer in the chest. They tussled and disappeared inside.

Within minutes, the Captain of the Turkish destroyer notified the Admiral that they were getting under way. Forty-five minutes later, the ship returned with the sailor, still in his messed-up clothes, hanging lifelessly from the yardarm. To eliminate any complications of Italian law, the Turks had sailed into International waters.

On hearing the news, Commander Kanakanui sat bolt upright and slammed the table. "Now, that's justice!"

Ens. Anthony controlled his impulse to jump up and shout, "No. damnit, it's not!"

Ode to a Green Bean

By Ida J. Lewenstein

Lean Bean
Green Bean
Clinging to the vine
The sun has kissed you
The rain has misted you
Soon you'll be mine, all mine.

Lean Bean
Green Bean
I've plucked you just in time!
You're ripe
And how!
You know
I can't wait 'till dinner time.

Now I clutch you
In my fingertips
Then draw you to my waiting lips
You're so tender, yet crisp
At last you're mine, all mine!

Munch.....crunch.....
Crunch........munch...
Ah.........
... So divine!

Liva and Let Liva

By Sue Barizon

I heard David Letterman tell this story on his late night talk show and laughed harder than I knew I should.

"A woman at a casino carries a bucket of her winnings onto an elevator occupied by two big black men. She becomes frightened, fearing she may be robbed. She then hears one of them say, "Hit the floor." She reacts as though she's about to be assaulted, flinging the contents of the bucket up over her head before dropping down on all fours. The man who spoke had simply asked what floor she was going to. All he'd done was offer to hit the button for her floor. She's embarrassed. The next day she receives some flowers along with a note from the black men saying it's the biggest laugh they'd had in years. The note is signed Michael Jordan and Eddie Murphy."

I pictured myself on all fours suspended over the floor of that elevator surrendering to my own preconceived prejudice. Yes, I am prejudiced, but only moderately so. The five minute "How Prejudiced Are You?" test I took online confirmed what I already knew. What do you expect from a first generation

Italian-American garbageman's daughter, raised in the San Francisco Bay Area during the turbulent 60s?

My earliest recollection of race differences came from the kitchen pantry. I was well acquainted with the smiling faces of Aunt Jemima and Uncle Ben. They shared a shelf with the likes of Betty Crocker, Gerber Babies, Chiquita Banana, and Chef Boyardee. Intuitively I knew I was Italian (my parents peppered their conversation with the language); these faces introduced me to a reality outside my homogenous suburban cocoon. One time I lined up the Aunt Jemima and Betty Crocker mixes side by side, and dared Papa to give his opinion on who was the better cook.

"C'mon," he grumbled waving off the challenge. Then, he eyed my bemused mother standing at the kitchen stove stirring a pot of polenta. He pointed a critical finger at Betty Crocker. "Not that one," he said. "She looks like your mother; she probably can't make toast, either."

As I grew, the kitchen table became the classroom for teaching family values, morals, and the nuances of prejudice starting with our own ranks. I heard the Sicilians dismissed as the "Blacks" of Italy, and the Genovese teased for their penny-pinching, likening them to the "Jews." The well-educated Italians who looked down their noses on the peasant stock from which we came were condemned as "know-it-alls."

My easygoing father had a "live and let live" philosophy. I often heard him use the expression when he sat at the kitchen table with his neighborhood buddies nursing their five o'clock highballs. I'd listen as the bull sessions progressed to more controversial topics of the day and inevitably became heated. The fervent switchback from English to Italian was confusing, but I was a seven-year-old sponge and soaked up the language of prejudice just the same.

I never heard the "N word" spoken in our house. Blacks were referred to as "Negre," Chinese as "Chin-e-say" and Jews as "Judah." To my senses, the Italian versions buffered the harshness of the English ones I heard on the playground. I learned to read the clues that spoke to the character of the men sitting around our table; the way Ernie Griffin averted his eyes when Tony Lucca joked about having neglected to tip the "Negre" parking attendant. How Frank Ricci gave a half-hearted chuckle and poured himself another shot. How Mario Lombardi laughed as he pilfered through his wallet and threw a dollar bill across the table at Tony, "For next time, you cheap son-of-a bitch!" Then my Uncle Pete's arbitrary "They got to eat, too." How Papa, with his hang-dog expression and perpetually broken English brought closure, "C'mon boys, liva and let liva."

Years later I learned about the pockets in Papa's prejudice. Dinnertime conversation often centered on his garbage route in San Francisco's Fisherman's Wharf. He told stories of the City in the wee hours and the misadventures shared with his partners Rico and Leoni. Papa touted the threesome's camaraderie, mutual respect, and good humor—a necessity for packing a forty-pound can up a flight of stairs and sidestepping rats the size of alley cats.

One night, after dinner, Papa produced a couple of photographs from his shirt pocket. They were taken by one of the customers on his route. The first photograph showed Papa with an easy smile sitting on the front bumper of a garbage truck. A slim built man with his arms folded and his cap brim turned up sat next to him. In the second photograph the same man posed standing in the open cab of the truck. A third man, square shouldered and proud sat next to the driver, my father, who was smiling playfully from behind the steering wheel.

"Who are these guys?" I asked Papa, pointing to the two black men.

Papa tapped their faces with a pointed finger. "That's Rico and that's Leoni."

"What?" I yelped. "I thought they were Italian!"

Papa gave my mother a dubious look. She had already seen the photographs and reacted with characteristic indifference to Papa's two black co-workers. "Susan, don't you know your father's English by now? Rico is Roscoe, Leoni is Leroy."

As a teenager growing up in the 60s, I'd monitor the telltale vein on Papa's neck bulge as he watched the six o'clock news. His blood pressure registered contempt as our generation practiced its version of freedom of speech. In his eyes, the race riots, demonstrations, and protests boiled down to disrespect for authority. However, it was the looting, physical assaults, and random destruction of property that provoked the strongest reaction from my "live and let live" father.

"You wanna march through the streets, go ahead, MARCH to Timbuktu!" Papa would bark at the TV. Next, he'd turn to us kids sitting at the table eating our dinner, and ask, "But why you wanna go break some poor guy's window and steal him blind?" Then, through clenched teeth he'd spew forth threats of his own violence aimed at the young radicals. "Dirty son-a-ma-baygos! They oughtta take a machine gun, line up against a wall and... eh, eh, eh, eh, eh, eh!" There was nothing like the evening news coupled with Papa's accented machine gun fire for venting hostility towards your fellow man.

You might say Papa got a taste of his own medicine the day I delivered it to him, second-hand. A boy I had been dating for two years had finally suggested I meet his parents. When he came to pick me up, he took me aside and broke the news that I wouldn't be meeting them after all.

"Why not?" I asked.

"Because my mother wanted to know what your father did for a living," he said. "I told her he was a garbage man."

It was the first time I could honestly say I'd experienced prejudice. Although I was the intended victim, I felt strangely protective of Papa. Incensed, I wasted no time in running to tell him all about the grave injustice that had been heaped upon both of us.

"Who does she think she is? I'm a cheerleader for Christ's sake and the sophomore class secretary. I have a 3.0. Her own son doesn't even have a 3.0! Her husband is a pasty-faced accountant, for crying out loud. You probably make twice the money he does." I ranted on, determined to show Papa how little it mattered to me. Papa listened as he sat in his Barca lounger, staring straight ahead, not swallowing or blinking. The telltale vein on his neck remained conspicuously inactive during my "moderately prejudice" tirade. When I was spent, he looked up at me with his hangdog expression and gently shrugged.

"C'mon now. Liva and let liva."

Chasing Carol Stein

By Lisa Meltzer Penn

I remember Carol Stein saying no one could ever expose or shame her, because she had nothing to hide, she was an open book.

But even a book has things to hide, undetected at first sight. Opening a book does not necessarily fan out its pages, all its layers of secret and artifice.

Just a face, not an artifice, Carol would say, grinning.

It had been a couple of years since college when I spotted Carol Stein between 21st and 22nd Streets on the west side of Manhattan. It was September, and I was walking home from work. Carol's familiar wavy red hair flowed down her back as she strolled with a friend.

I quickened my pace, thinking to catch up and surprise her, but the two of them were faster than me. We continued through the construction scaffolding that formed a dark tunnel on 23rd. On the sidewalk, something dank and oily had formed a shallow puddle. I didn't like to think what. Along with the other pedestrians, I tried to sidestep the wet spot, but it didn't slow down Carol.

At the corner, Carol turned left, her red mane swinging to the side. Her friend's sleek bob glinted for a moment above her animal print scarf. Forsaking my usual route, I followed them, getting caught up in a line of people waiting to cross at the light. Carol and her friend slipped easily through the crowd, chattering obliviously as I tried to catch up.

I envisioned myself darting in front of Carol and yelling, *Surprise!*

Carol was one of those people who was nice to everyone. A year older than me, we had shared a suite in our dorm with two other girls. Carol was the one who had directed me to the more interesting freshman philosophy seminars, and cheered me up with a pint of mint chocolate chip the first time I got dumped.

I was losing her, so I started to jog, squeezing around the oncoming pedestrians, brushing against a big man who stepped in front of me and leered. I inched around him and continued walking.

What did I expect Carol's response to be? Joy, of course. She would be thrilled to see me. There would be a cry of delight, a warm hug, a promise to get together soon. Then a quick exchange of numbers and a heartfelt see-you-later. Wasn't that how chance encounters went? I was already looking forward to having coffee or lunch.

Finally, I gave up trying to navigate the crowd. "Carol! Carol Stein!" I called.

But we were in yet another scaffolding tunnel and my voice didn't carry well.

Carol's hand reached back, brushing her hair momentarily from her neck. I couldn't quite see her face, just the curve of cheek before the hair dropped back. But I remembered her face—freckled nose, rounded cheeks, twinkling eyes.

I abandoned all pretense of surprise. "Carol!" I called again more loudly. "Hey, Carol, hold up!"

She stopped and turned toward me. I had managed to get closer and I saw her face full-on now. She looked annoyed. I didn't know why. It caught me off-guard. "Carol?" I said again. "Carol Stein?" She frowned. Then she turned away and kept walking.

"Carol?" I repeated loudly.

She stopped and turned again, hand on her hip, looking me over. "I'm *not* Carol Stein," she said.

I stood in the mingle of people, not knowing what to do. She looked just like Carol Stein. Not only the hair or the shape of her cheek, but every feature of her face. Yet she regarded me as though I were a stranger.

"You're not?" I asked dumbly. How could I have made such an error?

"No," she snapped. "I'm not that person. You're mistaken."

I looked to Carol's friend for confirmation. She was a petite Asian woman, Filipino if I had to guess, in a fashionable black dress and that print scarf. She raised her eyebrows, examining me shrewdly for a moment, and shrugged. Then the two women turned and walked away.

Was Carol's face different? Was I remembering her wrong? Did she possibly have amnesia? Or was she really not Carol Stein? But then, who was she to carry the same hair, the same face? She looked exactly as I'd remembered.

I watched until I could no longer see the bounce of her red hair. Turning the other way, I zigzagged the blocks and avenues toward home, stopping when I had to wait for the flashing red sign to change to the white-light icon of the walking man.

Where was my Carol Stein if this person was not her? This person who had no memory of me. Carol had never mentioned an identical twin. And if she were a sister of any kind, the name Carol Stein would not have struck her as foreign and obtrusive. For who would disown friendly Carol?

I had not thought much about my Carol Stein in the years since college. I could have searched her out and probably found her. Apparently she lived in Manhattan now, too. Or, at the least, this other Carol Stein did. But that's the thing about chance encounters: they are subject to unwritten rules. Was my old friend not the open book she had professed to be? Was she harboring major secrets?

Perplexed, I stopped at the traffic light, waiting for it to change. With the press of bodies gathering force around me, I began to see that the rules of fate could turn the corner as well. For never offering up that moment of reunion, for never bringing into being that person or thing you lacked, the molten object or past that lay just out of reach.

Old Light and Indifference

By Bill Baynes

Aboard the timeliner
As it sails across Belmont
The traffic is tidal
And the waves keep the clock
The years on this deck
I have seen many things
I have been many men

A student, a pauper
A leader, an achiever
I have seen the glances
Idea man, conceiver
I have had my chances
I have been a father
I have been a believer

A twelve-year-old boy
Before the secret world opens
And nuns with rulers rule
Jesus and suffering
I give up comics for Lent

FAULT ZONE: Transform

Say novenas after supper
On my knees to the radio

I recall my children as children
My parents alive and strong
Times of uncertainty, ecstasy
But now I can't remember
The meal I ate yesterday
The book I said I'd never forget
Today's memory is a memory

Standing in the ocean
I'm lifting off my feet
Daring the sweepaway
Risk is a toy, a bauble
Gambles and adventures
Repeated business failures
Always almost there

Age is inlaid with sorrow
The more of one, the more
The other, the brothers
Missing, the missions undone
I'm older by the hour
But timeships never dock

FAULT ZONE: Transform

And this night's so young

It's starry and still
And smells wonderful
The kind of night
You can almost sense
The planet's dervish dance
The sky full of old light
And indifference

Cal "The Intellecta" Critbert In

The Sinister Soul Surfer!

By Dave M. Strom

My Intellecta-phone vibrated, disturbing my review of the movie sequel, *My Introspective Winter in Montegood Mansion*. It was a police supervillain alert: SEASIDE FIRST COASTAL VAULT BREACHED BY HARRY HEADBUTT AT 11:37:05 A.M. HELP! I summoned my Intellecta-car via my telepathic link. I dashed out of the Pacific Theater complex and dived into the open passenger door of my big, black, scary, crime-fighting vehicle. I pulled my black, bulletproof costume, cape, and cowl from below the car seat and wrestled into it. Meanwhile, my car auto-piloted me to the bank, zipping around and leaping over traffic where the super-carpool lane was unavailable. My sweet, super-strong Holly had surely received the same message on her e-bracelet. She could fly. She'd get there first.

•

Anxious minutes later, I ran into the bank lobby and thundercloud-billowed my cape, making cringing civilians step aside. I bounded over broken mahogany loan officer desks and unconscious cops, and dashed toward the prone supervillain, Harry Headbutt. The fake muscles sculpted into my body armor were no protection against muscles that had torn off the eight-foot wide bank vault door. I drew my Intellecta-gun, screaming "Holly, he's getting up! I need your super-strength NOW!"

Seven-foot-tall and five-foot-wide of torn-pants-and-nothing-else clad man-mountain glowered down at me. His biceps bulged. His cauldron belly quivered. His sweat stung my Intellecta-sense of smell. I stood before him. Alone.

Cameras clicked. Paparazzi hooted. Super Holly Hansson posed and preened in her heroic blue supersuit and red cape. *Why wasn't she helping me?*

I aimed my Intellecta-gun. Eighteen percent chance that my prototype Harry-Headbutt-buster bullet would stun Harry, 82 percent he'd spit it back. Odds that rotten worked only in the movies.

But Harry just pouted. He crossed gorilla arms over battleship-armor pectorals and sat down on the floor with a meaty **THUMP**. "HARRY WANT LAWYER!"

I repressed laughter at his resemblance to the star of *Terror of the Titanic Toddler* (three stars). "So you didn't rob the bank?"

Harry huffed, a steam engine sneeze. "NO! HARRY TOOK DAY OFF. WENT TO BEACH AND BUILT SAND CASTLE. STUPID SURFER KICK IT. HARRY LIFT FIST TO SMUSH! THEN HARRY HERE." He swung his puffy face toward the bent vault door, smashed furniture, scared bank employees, and black-eyed, bloody-nosed cops stumbling to their feet. "HARRY MISSED GOOD TIME."

I whipped out my Intellecta-phone and hacked into the bank's surveillance video. "Let's review that."

Cops gathered around the 3D hologram playing above my phone. Movie violence always fascinates.

In the hologram, Harry swatted cops with a cry of "Cowabunga!" Not his usual bellow of "PUNY COPS!"

The bank front doors crashed open. My beloved Holly, first on the scene, missiled at Harry, her right fist surrounded by a transparent, super-strength enhancing, telekinetic shield. "Nap time, butt-head!"

Harry smiled gleefully. "I'm catchin' those curves!" Harry never referred to himself in first person!

Like a ghost from The Body Grabbers *(one star), a swimsuited teenage boy leaped out of Harry and into Holly.* My super-intellect recalled the thousands of faces in the superpowers database and got—oh no. Bobby Breaker. The Soul Surfer. Why couldn't ghosts be real, instead of this idiot?

Harry fell into Holly's fist. And plopped to the floor.

Holly smiled gleefully. She put her foot on Harry's chest and her hand on her thigh. Her supersuit was the bare-leg variety. "I'm lovin' these curves!"

I returned my phone to my utility belt. I knew that Harry had been surfed.

So had Holly. She twirled and twerked, kicked cheerleader high, and flipped her long blonde hair for, as she usually put it, pervy paparazzi. One zoomed on

Holly's breasts, disobeying her yellow up-arrow chest logo. He crowed, "I need a wide angle lens!"

Holly crowed, "Get my good sides!" More out of character than Rocky "The Bicep" Roberts in *Crazy Cross-Dressing Cheerleaders* (one star), Holly put her hands under her breasts and lifted. Over a year ago, when she had acquired her superpowers, she had simultaneously acquired a super-bosom. She was still testy about the latter.

Her teeth bared. "rrrRRR!"

She let go fast, blinking fire out of her eyes and hope out of my heart. I read her lips: "Gnarly."

Harry frowned at Holly and said, "YELLOW HAIR NOT YELLOW HAIR."

"No, really, yah think?" said a female cop. She asked me, "Mr. Critbert, you need help with your girlfriend?"

"No. Make sure no one follows us." While constructing a mental prison cell, I sidled up to Holly and whispered, "The Soul Surfer wants you. Only I know this. We must hide!"

Holly smirked like a villain about to murder the hero. "Sure, dude."

•

In idiot plot movies, girls go into dark alleys with suspicious guys. Holly had macho-strutted into this alley, leaned against a dumpster, and smacked her fist into her palm over and over. "So only you know?"

I whipped Holly's main weakness out of my utility belt and stiff-armed it toward her. "Yes, I know!"

She slumped to her knees. Her face paled in a green glow. Her big blue eyes poured betrayal into mine. "Why?"

My heart broke, my mind didn't. Holly had always insisted that as her dark knight, I carry her kryptonite. Green super-lutefisk in a sealed test tube. I had recently tasted plain lutefisk. For the remainder of my days, I'd wish I didn't have a photographic memory. I loomed over Holly—or rather, Bobby/Holly—and dropped my voice an octave. "Get out of my girl!"

Bobby/Holly's face turned seasick green. "But I'm totally Holly!"

Anger reassembled my heart. "No, Bobby, you're a lousy actor!"

I held the glowing green tube closer as Bobby/Holly crawled back like a dying spider and scrunched next to a steel door in the alley wall. Superheroine legs rippled like slugs, a beautiful face became a pale skull. I hated being Lex Luthor.

Bobby/Holly put his hand over his mouth. "I think," *hiccup,* "I'm gonna hurl." He swallowed. "You win. I'll—"

I didn't see the steel door fly open and hit my hand: I'd lovingly and foolishly focused only on Holly. The tube flew at and clinked off the dumpster, rolled on grimy pavement, and fell down a storm drain.

Reverse deus ex machina. The unforeshadowed plot bomb. I hated when dead teenager movies killed just-had-sex teenagers with it. Hated when *Stumbling Corpse* movie finales insulted my intelligence with it. Hated hated hated it invading my real life.

A hunched old Popeye of a janitor tossed broken barbells into the dumpster. Must be a super-gymnasium next door. He peered at me and rasped, "Sorry 'bout dat, bat boy! Need help?"

"NO!" I shoved the janitor through the door and slammed it shut. Bobby mustn't catch another wave!

Bobby/Holly got up. No green in his cheeks, just healthy Swedish pink. He bodybuilder-flexed—"I'm stoked!—and threw a punch.

I casually leaned left. Bobby had Holly's body, but he didn't have her boxing skills. Next to my head, a blue-clad arm plowed into the dumpster up to the elbow.

My chances of saving Holly were nil. So I punched Bobby/Holly in the nose.

"Ow!" Bobby/Holly pulled his arm out of the wall and gaped at me. "How come that hurt? You only got normal strength!"

"Then have a normal knuckle sandwich." I punched rosy red, super-strong, pillow soft lips. I kept my expression grim despite guilt twisting my gut.

Bobby/Holly charged with all the finesse of a bull. My Intellecta-judo redirected him onto an alley wall. Then the other wall. Then the dumpster. Olé.

Yes! A twitch in Bobby/Holly's right eyelid, Holly hated when I used her super-strength against her! I grabbed long silky hair—Holly loathed that—and threw Bobby/Holly into a big patch of cobwebbed alley ivy.

Holly was fearless. But she could be creeped out. She clawed spiders and webbing off her arms, face, and hair: "Ew, ew, ew, ew, EW!"

No! Bobby/Holly's stupid squint returned! "Whoa! She almost woke up!" He strutted toward me, fist cocked. "You're going to sleep!"

Anger and revulsion had failed. So I leaned into the punch. My soulmate connection with Holly prevented her super-strength from harming me. But Holly was six-foot-one and she loved me, her writing, and her punching bag, not always in that order. Her normal strength packed a wallop.

I saw stars. I said, "You hit like a girl."

My split lip and my right eyelid swelled as Bobby/Holly pummeled and yelled, "Why aren't I smashing you?"

Same soulmate reason I punched you without breaking my hand, stupid. My Intellecta-stamina kept me standing. I scrutinized my assailant: eyelids twitching, pupils dilating, lips trembling. Holly's heart was breaking!

Bobby/Holly stepped back and blinked hard. "Down, DOWN!" He glared at me. "I know what you're doing! I'm outta here!" With a Superman pose that perfectly suited Holly, Bobby/Holly flew straight up.

Time for Chekhov's shotgun rule! I drew my Intellecta-gun and fired. Bobby/Holly ping-ponged between alley walls and plowed into the dumpster in a tangle of red cape, blue-clad arms, blonde hair, and long legs. *WHAT HAD I DONE?*

Logic left me. I ran to her. "Holly! Speak to me!"

A six-foot transparent hand punched out of the dumpster and slammed me against the wall. Bobby/Holly ogled how it extended from his outstretched left arm. "Tubular!"

Bobby/Holly's right hand held a fifty-pound dumbbell. My soulmate connection wouldn't protect...both should hear this.

"Bobby. If you punch me with that, the momentum will pulverize my skull. I will die by Holly's hand. Do you really want that?"

The dumbbell aimed the dumbbell. "Yeah! Any last words?"

I cast my heart into Holly's big blue eyes. "I love you, Holly."

The dumbbell rushed forward. And stopped a millimeter from my nose.

"Huh?" Bobby/Holly punched and stopped again.

The fist dropped the dumbbell. Turned toward Bobby/Holly's face. Reared back. And ... **KA-POWWW!!!**

My heart sang. Holly was back! And swinging!

Like in the movie *Doctor Strangelove* where Peter Sellers grabbed at his seig-heil saluting arm, Bobby/Holly's left hand flailed at Holly's jackhammering right fist. He inverted the bully's battle: "Stop hitting yourself!" **POW POW!** "Stop hitting yourself!" **POW POW POW!** "STOP ..." **POW POW POW POW!** "HITTING ..." **POW POW POW POW POW!** "YOURSELF!"

His bloody-nosed, split-lipped face morphed from mouth breathing to Holly's lioness growling. "Get out of my body, you TWERP!"

Bobby/Holly's left hand caught Holly's right wrist. He grinned. "No!"

Holly snarled. Her right hand lunged, clamped onto her beaky nose, and twisted with a Three Stooges **KERRRRUNCH!** Holly liked the ones with Curly.

Bobby/Holly's eyes crossed. "Ooo! Ooo! OOOOOO!!!"

Holly let go. "Had enough?"

I yelled, "Don't let up! You've got him on the ropes!"

Holly snapped, "Shut up, this is ..." She staggered. "my ... fight ... uhhhh."

Eyes squished shut. Arms stiffened. "Down, you're going down, DOWN, **DOWN!**" Bobby/Holly's eyes opened, triumphant and cruel. "There!" His hands roamed Holly's thighs and butt. "Mmm, yeah! She's out!"

I winced. "Do you have to do that?"

"Yeah! I like hot babes!" Bobby/Holly looked down. Again his stupid smile on Holly's lips. "Are these double-Ds?"

It took all my hundreds of I.Q. points not to smile. "Triple."

Bobby/Holly groped and squeezed. "*COWABUNGA!!!*"

"*rrrrRRRRROWL*!!!" Holly let go, grabbed her left little finger, and yanked it before her face.

Bobby/Holly's jaw dropped. "You wouldn't dare!"

Holly wrenched the finger back. The snap flipped my stomach.

Bobby/Holly hopped like an electroshocked cheerleader. "You're crazy!"

Holly shrieked through gritted teeth, "No!"

A punch in her mouth: ***THOOM!*** "I!"

Fingers in her eyes: ***DOINK!*** "Am!"

A hand on her throat: "***ANGRRRYYY!!!***"

A purple-faced Bobby/Holly gurgled, "I'm outta here."

Holly crumpled to the dingy ground. A surfer dude flew out of her and toward me. "Say goodbye to your body!"

At last! I opened my mind and swallowed.

Holly dragged herself to her feet, panting like an Amazon after battle. She plodded toward me. The liquid sway of her hips had returned. "Cal, are you—"

SWOOSH went my cape as I strode forward and swept my Wonderful Woman into my arms. I kissed her, avoiding her surely painful proboscis. "Holly, are YOU all right?"

She moaned, "I'd love an iced mocha." She jolted and backed off, her face a frowning rainbow of black, blue, orange, purple, and red. She scanned left, right, over her shoulder, back to me. "Where is he?"

I tapped my cranium.

Oops. Holly grabbed my shoulder with her left hand and hissed in pain. She aimed her right fist. "Let Cal go!"

I raised my hands in please-don't-hit-me posture. "Holly! I trapped Bobby in my mind! He's a BB in a boxcar! I'm Cal!"

Holly's gaze was deadly. "Prove it."

I rose to my full five-foot-eleven, spread my cape into dark wings, and filled my eyes with Dracula.

Holly's eyes went dreamy. Her lips plumped into want-to-be-kissed-some-more. And her facial bruises faded. FAST!

I yanked her finger into place and twisted her nose back five minutes.

"*OWWWITCH!*" Holly flexed her fist, crossed her eyes at her nose, and sniffed. "You're Cal, all right. Warn me next time!"

I pulled a hanky from my utility belt and wiped blood off her beautiful face. "Sorry, I had to set your bones before they super-healed. Now hold still ... hold STILL!"

Holly fussed like I'd spit on the hanky. "You're messing up my lip gloss! I—" She gasped, touched my split lip, and stared at my blood on her fingertip. A tear ran down her cheek. Her face went ashen. "I hurt you."

This was the same woman who, during last week's sparring session, screamed that she'd rip my arm off and stuff it somewhere very uncomfortable if I didn't stop throwing her twenty feet whenever she threw a right hook at me.

I kissed her nose. "Bobby did it, not you."

Her tears rivered from twin oceans of sorrow. "I'm so sorry."

I whipped out a tube of Intellecta-ointment and dabbed my lip. "This will make me better."

Supple arms wound around me. Lips that could dent steel caressed mine. "Let me make you more better."

I kissed her. "You realize that this has no medicinal value?"

She kissed my right eye. It felt better.

Hmm. "I also value my mouth."

She hugged me closer, soft and strong. Her lips merged with mine. Strawberry lip gloss tingled my taste buds. She pawed back my cowl and ran her fingers through my hair. She kissed my cheek, neck, forehead, left eye, right ear—MMM-WAH!—left ear twice—MMM-WAH! MMM-WAH!—and her smile warmed my heart. "You're distracted, aren't you?"

I nodded. "You know me so well. 5.2 percent of my intellect is dispensing justice to a surfer." I put darkness in my voice. "Artsy-fartsy justice."

Holly's eyes flared with fangirl glee. "That's so...Batman!"

•

Inside the movie theater I had constructed within my massive mind, my movie playback skipped a frame. Holly was getting frisky.

"Lemme out, pleeeeeease? This movie sucks!" whined Bobby. He was stuck in a theater seat, his eyes Clockwork Orange glued to the screen.

Next to him, I leaned back and drank a soliloquy about red velvet living room drapes. *My Philosophical Autumn in Montegood Mansion* offered more with every viewing. "Enjoy a little culture. I'll adjust my mental timeline so that we can watch it five more times before I drop you off at super-jail."

That's when I slapped a mental gag on Bobby, cutting off his scream.

Again. Again.

By Frank A. Saunders

Spring conceals its cruelty
far beneath its daffodils.
Below the verdant frailty
an ancient, restless movement builds.

The residue of buried roots,
of tangled tendrils left to rot,
still holds the moldy skin of fruits
that long ago have withered. Fraught

with memory, they stir again.
Unbidden, they begin to grow
and choke the fragile shoots. Spring rain
gives life to bones from long ago.

We return to cut the weed
that threatens every nascent seed.

A Few Thoughts on Grief

By Ann Foster

Who knew we could make choices on how we grieve?

Until about a year ago, most of my griefs were tied up with the loss of an animal. These griefs taught me a lot about grieving for the loss of a friend. Not that I hadn't lost friends or family members before, but all those losses were preceded by long and often painful declines. Those came with sadness but also relief.

The loss of my horses was more shocking. Two years ago, I made the decision to put my beloved horse, Tribute, to sleep. My husband and I had made the decision jointly to do the best we could to save him, but to face the hard choice if it became obvious nothing could be done for him.

I had lost another horse twenty years before, and a horse dying is a shocking event, impossible to get your head around. I had no way to prepare. Sasha looked normal—no outward signs of injury—until she collapsed suddenly, spinning and falling in a swirl of dust. In my absence she had fallen against a metal pipe fence and cracked a vertebra high in her neck. The vet said she would never be safe to work around and certainly not safe to ride, as her seizures were incurable. I went home to talk to my husband, but the decision had been made for us. I spent the next six months in a kind of fog. I thought horses were out of my life forever. Guilt and sorrow threatened to overwhelm me.

When we had to make the same decision for Tribute, we'd had a month of watching him struggle, with tantalizing hints he might be getting better, only to have our hopes dashed. Again, the decision had been made for us. We called the vet, prepared Tribute for his final walk with a massive dose of pain killer, groomed him till he gleamed, and waited for death to arrive in the form of an injection of barbiturates.

This time, I was better prepared, though 'prepare' is not the best word here. I knew I would grieve, but I also knew that Tribute was in such pain that I could let go of the guilt and do the right thing with love. I cried a lot. But I also had a great good-bye. At some point, he gave me permission to let him go with gladness. As we shared our final morning, I made a choice. I was not going to isolate myself from horses as I had when Sasha died. If I chose to love another horse, it would not mean I loved him less.

Now I have lost two people very precious to me, but having loved *them*, means I love more, not less. I think of them often, without pain, remembering all that they gave to the world. Yes, I grieve, but I remember them with gladness. My life is richer because I loved them and my grief is healthier because I practiced with my horses.

Sweet Harmony

By TR Poulson

The fiery dark bay colt's neck and mane quivered like molten lava between Todd's hands. Storms had drenched the track that morning, and when the sun emerged, temperatures soared. Certainly, the conditions didn't treat hangovers so well. Or was he still drunk? He couldn't remember clunking his last empty bottle down on the counter, returning home at dawn, or falling into his twin bed for a few hours before dragging himself to Del Mar. In the first race he'd been a mere passenger as his maiden filly tucked herself onto the rail, stalked the leaders, and lost by a length.

Now, in the starting gate for the fourth race, he tried to calm the dark bay colt, Play Action. He'd been excited to be given the mount on this high-strung son of A. P. Indy. As the colt fidgeted between his feet, Todd tried to piece together his trainer's instructions: he tends to be slow at the break; let him settle into his pace. What else? This lightly-raced colt was better than anything else he was riding that day, even his Pacific Classic horse. Not drunk, he told himself. Tired. His hand quivered up to his face to adjust his goggles.

The dark bay colt stumbled out the gate, and hindquarters converged in front of them. Fuck. Play Action didn't like having dirt flipped in his face. Todd struggled to breathe. And then he felt that uneven stride, followed by another, another. He pulled the reins, hard, as the colt's head dropped and he tumbled into the dirt. Steel-shod hooves hurdled around him, over him. Later, in the hospital, he learned they had to put the colt down, right there on the track.

Todd watched the replay video, and then refused to see it again. He tried to delete the memories, the images of that fiery colt, from his head.

Play Action, owned and named by a football fan, sired by the great A. P. Indy, appeared destined for the classics—until that race. But there was a dark side to his pedigree. His dam was a full sister to the filly who'd been euthanized in the Kentucky Derby all too recently. This is what racing fans posted about on Facebook. None of it mattered to Todd. He tried to forget other things: Play Action loved oatmeal cookies. When bored, he would paw the shavings in his stall or grab the hats off passers-by. He tossed his head, and when he did, the star on his forehead, shaped like an exclamation point, would dance like a pogo stick.

In Todd's dreams, Play Action floundered in recurring seas of blood.

•

He quit drinking. All of it—the suicidal thoughts, the meetings—would be documented in a short film which would air six years later on a Friday night in May, the night before the Run for the Roses. In interviews, he would talk about the warm fuzzy stuff, like finding his estranged daughter, and about how she motivated him to stay away from booze. All of it would be true, but he would never tell them about the ghost which stalked him.

It first appeared when Todd had been six months sober. At his buddy's wedding, he hid in the bathroom during the toast. He stood up after pretending to take a dump, and as he was washing his hands, the dark bay ghost pranced in behind him in the mirror and tossed its head. The creature's eyes glowed as though he were just a bit stoned, his forelock whipped around his ears and the sliver of a star on his forehead. His nostrils spread like a dragon's, and he arched his neck like a dressage horse. Todd turned to face him, looked down, and choked back a scream. One of the forelegs dangled like a broken whip.

He took a breath and closed his eyes. When he opened them, the ghost was still there. He tried to touch the ghost's face, but his hand went right through it. Why, then, could he feel warm breath against his cheek? The ghost followed him out to the party, where Todd paused for a long moment at the bar, then found the bowl of fruit punch. No alcohol, the server said.

The ghost horse disappeared.

In the following weeks and months, the ghost showed up at odd moments: as he dressed for AA meetings, after a date, at work. After he lost his jockey's license, one of his girlfriends had found him a job at a warehouse. The ghost pawed the concrete and pirouetted around pallets as Todd stacked boxes on them, labels facing out, to be scanned.

•

Five years sober, Todd dreamed he sat astride a chestnut filly in the gate. The crisp air filled his lungs, and clouds lurked. The filly radiated a strange warmth. He looked out at the first turn, framed by her ears, and then the gate sprung open. They broke cleanly, led into the first turn, hugged the rail. The clouds fell like fog, and the track disappeared into a field of mist.

She took him everywhere: through lightning, snowstorms, sunsets, rainbows, and star-filled skies. She filled him with her power, her strength, her heart, and took him to visit golden fields where long-gone champions grazed. He looked back, and saw her competitors far behind. Her hooves kicked wildflowers into sparkly dust.

A mountain appeared, first tiny on the horizon, then bigger and bigger until it loomed so large it might topple on them, but they found a trail. She took him up the switchbacks, until the stone wall gave way to a field of roses. The roses surrounded them like faces in the stands. Their scents took him into their world. She faltered and fell to her knees.

He dismounted. The thorns had torn her flesh apart. Rivulets of blood flowed from her legs and belly, into the ever-present roses. A pool of blood engulfed her, and she vanished.

•

Todd's daughter—conceived in a drunken adventure, supported with checks for six years before he contacted her as a part of AA's step eight—talked him into riding again. She was already quite the little horsewoman, and posters of dressage horses covered her bedroom walls. She added one of Rosie Napravnik, in the Kentucky Oaks.

Todd started exercising horses at Golden Gate Fields.

In a dream, his little girl, aged into a young woman, rode Play Action to a Breeders' Cup victory. In the winner's circle, the colt turned his head to Todd, and the star on his face lengthened into a blaze. He jolted awake, and the ghost horse stood over him.

"Leave my daughter alone," he begged the ghost, and tried to shove it away, but his hands felt nothing. The beast watched him shave, and then trotted behind him to the track. At the tack room, the ghost asked for an oatmeal cookie. Todd looked everywhere for one, and finally found one in the bottom of a tack trunk. It was moldy.

The ghost stuck his head through the door and shook it, as if laughing. He stepped back and did the *piaffe*, a trot-in-place move that Todd recognized from his daughter's videos. Todd looked down. The ghost's leg wasn't broken, had never broken. He dropped the cookie and it shattered in the dust. You see, the colt seemed to say with his eyes, you always fuck up. It wouldn't have happened with a different jock. A sober one.

•

An up and coming owner gave him the mount on a strange filly named Sweet Harmony, a golden chestnut with a wide blaze and four long stockings. She reminded him of someone, but he told himself he didn't want to know her. She moved like a robot and held her head almost still, as though she didn't want to disturb a hair in her forelock. Her dark, mysterious eyes pulled him into her, and told him, I Don't Want to Run. Well, it would be a short career for her, then.

But run, she did. She hesitated at the break, as her trainer warned him she would. Her muscles seemed to join with his as she stalked the field, her ears pricked, her face seemingly oblivious to the dirt being kicked onto it. His whole body became an extension of her: his hands, his legs, even his mind. He let the magic flow as he guided her between horses. He talked to her in familiar ways: a touch of the heel, a brush with the whip, a squeeze of a finger. But somehow, with her, it felt different. She took the lead and outdistanced her rivals.

He rode her again, with similar results. After the third straight victory, Todd was asked to ride her at Santa Anita. He looked at her wide-blazed face, her curved ears that indicated the "big heart" gene, her body, built and conditioned to win. None of these things motivated him to accept. Her eyes followed him. He dropped his whip. She was the chestnut filly from the field of roses.

He said yes.

The ghost said no. He followed Sweet Harmony on the track one day as the exercise rider worked her and Todd watched from the rail. As he limped along behind her, his foreleg dangled useless once again. In spite of his handicap, he stalked the filly and bit her tail. Sweet

Harmony seemed not to notice him at all, her ears pricked as she breezed five furlongs.

As the filly's groom bathed her, the ghost taunted her. He rode up onto his hind legs in the *levade*. His only body movement was the back and forth swing of his broken foreleg. Time slowed. As the ghost's body stood partially suspended, Todd looked closely at the sliver of a star on his face. It was bent and unbroken. Holy shit. He closed his eyes and tried to picture Play Action, alive. His star was straight, and broken into an exclamation point. He was certain of it. And, how could he have forgotten that Play Action was a front-runner, not a stalker?

"You're not the A. P. Indy colt," he almost screamed. "You're not the horse I killed. You're not Play Action."

The ghost lowered his forelegs and galloped away.

•

How strange to be back at Churchill for the Kentucky Oaks, Sweet Harmony as his mount. Last night his daughter had asked him why he'd decided to return with the filly to big time racing. He said, "I did it for you, honey." It wasn't a lie. Not really. But how could he explain the magic of the filly, the power of her?

The girl asked about Play Action.

"It was my drunk riding that killed him."

She surprised him. "No. I read about his pedigree. His dam was a full sister to Eight Belles."

Yes. He knew that. But that gimpy Raise A Native blood flowed in many thoroughbreds, and not all of them broke down on the track. "We'll never know, for sure, honey. I can only control what I do."

Later, something jolted him wide-awake. He remembered his dream about the filly, and he saw the end of it clearly. As the blood flowed from her, she rose back to her hooves on unbroken legs. Her wounds were only surface scrapes.

The Last Time I Met Myself

By Michele Jessen

The last time I met myself I was standing on our
       sailboat
One hand on the stanchion, the other on my hip
My smile deep and proud
A photo staring back at me from the draped dining
       room table

Lost at the dress store, hiding among the costumes
I slide into another body, not my own
but of the makings and trappings of wrapping paper
Painting money and labels on my skin
Arms extending out grow heavy
       burdens of wealth and pride piercing my
       exposed heart.
My tongue speaks of a wife that cannot be me
My hair dyed grows long, my nails bit short

Where am I? I am long gone

In memory, I speak to myself of trophies
San Mateo County Junior Olympics, age ten
Beating my arms through the wind
Pumping air at my side, running in the race
Hair flying backward, chest forward, legs extended
Wining yes, wining
My father cheering from the stands

shadow of my mother

Decades later
I catch glimpses of myself and try to hold on
Calling to myself
Begging myself, stay stay
Please live here again with me
I just found myself

I want to stay, remain here
Watching myself win the race again and again and
      again

Yet I hide under the covers
Back to sleep, always a forced slumber
Pushing tight the folds of blankets
Pressing eyelids into themselves

I exist in my dreams
There I am free. I walk, I run. Simply me
Unaware of my outer appearance
A place without time

Escaping aging
Outrunning the heaviness that follows me when I wake
My Dad, years gone to the grave
My trophy entombed, tarnished in the darkened casket

Keep it for me Dad. Hold onto the days long past
When I ran through your camera's click
When a fleeting photo was fresh and quick

FAULT ZONE: Transform

Hundreds of slides buried, now closeted
Dust grows and piles upon your windowless hoard
Waiting to be held up, perchance in years to come
To be dug out, lovingly lifted in hands
Hands of the little girl racing in the pictures

Holding out the mirror of skewed reality
Well done. How did you do that? Was that really you?
I cried, yet I don't know why. Goodbye moment

Time collects and sweeps into the dustbin
I scream for my memory notes to stay
Yet thousands of hours later,
They only stand together when no one is looking

The last time I saw myself I was not there
It was me...yet I was old...my loved ones gone

I reached up in the attic of my soul
I pulled down boxes of slides that poured over my head
Spilled onto the floor, surrounded my steps
Should I bend over and pick them up, or leave them
         where they lay?
For here come the vultures of time, picking through,
Discarding what only I hold dear

My winning trophy
My image caught running in track
My sailing days steering the boat

All rocks back and forth, repeating
I am here somewhere, repeating

FAULT ZONE: Transform

Hold on

Am I dreaming? Is this real?
They throw these objects overboard
Toss this. She won't need this anymore
What is this? There is not room for that

All sinks deeper in the ocean, fading beneath the water
While here I sail above, waving to the sinking objects
        of my past
Yearning to rescue them again. Save them. Keep safe
        what is mine
Yet if I sink with them, I will not stand
Struggle not, it will all be over soon

And so to sleep
Rest deep below the cool water, keep for me what lasts
Hold together dear trophy, until at last your edges rust
        and crumble
I will see you in my dreams
Sing sweetly reverie's aria, from the sunken grave
Flash cloud pictures, win the race against the wind for
        me

Do it for me, for I cannot
The last time I saw myself, I was not me
I was not here on earth, I was not

Circles

By Beverly Kalinin

I take today's little green pill with the bottled water I have purchased and notice that everything in this large, barrel-shaped food court is round. That comforts me, because circles connect, better than spirals can with their undesignated endings, which offer no solace. Rather, I need closure. "I want to feel enclosed." Did I really say that out loud? I take a quick glance around. They're all in their own cocoons.

I'm on a two-hour layover on my way to see family. I sip creamy clam chowder and feel warmed, then nurtured sitting beneath this high circular ceiling with its gentle recessed lighting tucked into half circles. Massive rounded pillars and beams extend to a centerpiece, a circular kiosk lighted all around. A tree grows in a wide, round bowl in the middle. It looks like a smoke stack on a ship. And the slated, wooden bench built all around it reminds me of a ship's railing, then of my husband's small fishing boat harbored in the Delta where the San Joaquin and Sacramento Rivers converge.

When he turned the key the boat's motor always made a loud noise then he, in his white tee shirt and baggy grays, would back it out of the berth, watching seriously over his shoulder. I would sit across at the small table and had to shout to speak. The ducks on the landing fluttered out of the way as he maneuvered the turn, honked to alert other crafts, and guided us out through the avenue of large and small vessels moored on either side. As we entered the wide expanse of the Delta, he honked again for no apparent reason. To me it seemed a happy announcement that he had been delivered once again to his favorite place. The bridge was a quarter mile to the right towards the vast network of sloughs, but we often stayed in the immediate area, circling slowly and wordlessly so he could determine, by observation of tide and wind, the best fishing spot for the day. The loud motor ceased then, the anchor held us, and soon the gentle slap, slap of the water and the whir of the fishing rod becalmed us.

Now, in this food court, I return to searching for more examples of the source of my contentment in this place. I see the hanging plants, tendrils of indoor greenery, spilling from wide, shallow round pots. The gray marble tables are round as well. People chat quietly, come and go, scrape the heavy wooden slate-backed chairs as they do so. For an hour I have been sitting at my table in one such sturdy, secure chair, which grounds me to this spot. I drag it a little closer to the table and enclose my shoulders with my jacket, wrapping the sleeves around in front. I leave my arms crossed there and commence to pat myself. I stop and glance left and right. I lower my hands to my lap, lean back, and allow myself to become absent-mindedly centered.

•

I think about having held my husband's hand for the landing a while ago. I imagine the familiar pressure he always exerted as the wheels touched down with a bump and the force of stopping roared in my ears. I always squeezed back. When I knew I was safe I allowed the thrill of the landing combined with my sweet memory of his hand to bring a smile to my face. I could feel the corners of my mouth rise up.

"Whoa, that was a jerk," the woman next to me had said when we landed today. I turned, still smiling, and nodded. She pushed her palms hard against the pants legs of her brown slacks that looked expensive.

"I am the original white-knuckle flyer," she apologized with a small laugh. She wore a ruby ring on her index finger and a diamond wedding set on the other hand. A gold bangle bracelet ringed one wrist.

"I know what you mean," I answered to be polite. She seemed about my age, seventy-ish. I was drawn to her gold loop earrings though they were flashier than I would wear. Her nails were flashy too, red and long. I wondered if it was uncomfortable for her to hold hands. I glanced at my own unadorned hands. They looked plain. I balled them into soft fists, hiding.

This was the first conversation we had had; perhaps it was prompted by her seemingly giddy relief at being landed. Now she was brushing lint or crumbs from her lap, those ringed hands flitting and glittering, the gold bracelet sliding up and down her arm.

"You don't seem nervous." She looked at me. "Actually, it's only the take-offs and landings I dread," she added.

I didn't tell her I have my husband's hand to hold on take-offs as well as landings. Once I read that married people live longer because of the constant touch of one another. When I read that I decided to go on holding my husband's hand. At quiet moments I practice doing so. I recall the muscular grip of that wide, solid hand. I feel it in mine.

The woman used her cell phone. "John, we're just taxiing in...yes, right on time." She snapped it closed and pulled out a compact and a tube of red lipstick.

In an airplane, when I sit on his right, I snuggle my left arm under his arm. And with my left hand I sort of latch onto his thumb from down under, palm on palm, with all my fingers hooked over his. And when I am sitting on the other side of him I do the same, grabbing onto his thumb while he embraces my whole hand around from the back where my baby finger is.

Sometimes on this side I can feel the pressure of his thin gold wedding band. And if I do not feel it, at least I am often looking at it, squeezed onto the fourth finger from which he traditionally never removed it. Fifty years and a bit tighter, the band remained. It fit loosely once when he was a slender twenty-one-year-old with a wide grin and horn-rimmed glasses. Every once in a while, he or I twirled the ring to make sure it still fit. It always did.

"It's a little tight," I would say.

"Yah," he'd answer in his agreeable way and test it himself, "but it's okay. It's good." Round and round he would twirl it.

•

I check the time. Twenty minutes to boarding. I would like a coffee but don't want to leave my secure, cozy spot. Instead I sip water. My husband, a Cancer sign, loved water as much as he did his boat. Not long ago I arranged for the harbor master to take me and my daughter out in the boat.

It was a clear, blue-sky day, with white clouds and warmish autumn breezes. The kind of day perfect for fishing, with the afternoon sun glistening on the calm water. The dirge-like low tones of the loud motor accompanied us as, from inside the cabin, the harbor master very, very slowly steered in a circle in the wide area outside the dock. Round and round we went. My daughter handed me the tin container with its heavy plastic sack of contents. Then she sat nearby on the motor box in the sun while I stood at the boat's side. Previously, I had cut the plastic strap from the sack. My tears flowed when I lifted the gray bag out and tipped it, allowing the dusty, coarse contents to pour slowly and evenly into the water. Peacefully, the ashes spread, as if with purpose and in slow motion. They were in no hurry to descend, but as they did so I sensed a mood of release and freedom. I could almost hear a satisfied "Ah!" as from one who finally rests at day's end.

I cried the whole time watching the beautiful whitish trail sink down. Nevertheless, I could breathe more easily knowing my husband was where he had wished to be at last. Until I stopped him, the harbor master continued to steer the boat two, three, maybe four times, circling us round and round and round.

Forgive the Changing Seasons

By Jo Carpignano

– 1 –
Autumn

Let's not blame Autumn for the waning light
as sunny Summer days begin to shrink
and fresh cool winds stir leaves about
Denigrated Autumn suffers poor rebuke,
when fruits ripened to their fullest–yield
rich red wines, sweet jams, and apple pies
As sudden turn of season chills the air
don't begrudge the onset of a colder clime
stop glorifying sweltering Summer sun
Let's celebrate instead the season's change
Exalt–as firmly anchored leaves transform
from drab indifferent green into a dazzling blaze
exploding into shades of ruby red and gold

– 2 –
Winter

Let's not blame Winter for the loss of Fall
When Autumn wore its brightest gown
it was seducing Winter from its dormancy

As winter winds blow strong and cold

FAULT ZONE: Transform

Fall was invited to release those gaudy leaves,
loosen ties, and liberate themselves in flight

Winter storms scatter Autumn glory, as bright
leaves swarm across the fields and sky in
flocks—as if pursuing phantom butterflies
And speak of beauty? Gaze upon the tree
bereft of leaves, standing naked in the snow
Observe its darkened silhouette against blue sky
Is it not perfect in its graceful symmetry?

− 3 −
Appreciate the Changes

Why should we not applaud chill Winter nights
and venerate the shorter days of Fall, when
long cold nights provide such needed rest
Extended hours during darkest night
allow time needed for mysterious events
like sleeping seeds that wait below the snow
Then, when Spring and Summer take their turn
the long night rest reveals those mysteries—
the hidden treasures brought to light
in warmer seasons' proud parade

The Dragon Smiles

By Don Redman

The warning shriek of slowly backing big rigs and parcel delivery vans blended seamlessly into the sights, sounds and frenzied motion of the main cargo terminal of Ronald Regan airport in Washington D.C. As the shabby old Kenworth trailer bumped the loading dock, the driver pushed in the clutch. He looked out of his grimy windshield at the dark winter's sky. The city's lights prevented heaven's stars from shining through. A pity. He looked down and checked his watch. Almost six-thirty, he still had time.

He leaned over, pulled the parking brake knob and took the transmission out of gear. Releasing the clutch he relaxed, closed his eyes and concentrated on his breathing, slow and steady, slow and steady. He sat quietly, feeling and listening to the engine idle before he shut it down for the last time.

Throughout the previous day he had seen ragged V formations of birds swim slowly across his windshield. Nature was such an endless wonder. He dropped his head and smiled a sad smile into the back of his hands. Despite the insanity of man, nature endures.

•

In Peking, commanding eyes searched for the true face of his people in the murals on the walls of this Great People's Hall. The Chairman's determined eyes passed slowly across the giant mural of strident committed workers, unwavering in their demands for a new path, for a new way. He turned to the opposite wall to valiant courageous soldiers and sailors defending the homeland. The Chairman examined each mural in turn. These inspirational Mao and Cultural Revolution era murals told great stories of great deeds and great sacrifice. But no matter the country no matter the era, strident militaristic uber patriotic themes always seemed to lack a spiritual or true inner view of a country's people. He pulled back his coat sleeve and looked down at his watch. He still had time.

The Chairman walked directly to his office. These political paintings were singular works, but he sought a different view of his people—a long view, a thousand year or Dynasty era type view, if you will.

The landscape was subtle, yet vast, in its scale and reach. Huge teal mountains shot up from fertile valleys. In the distance, a flock of birds in a ragged V formation flew towards the mountains. In the foreground, a white crane stood vigilant watch over verdant forests and thundering waterfalls. This was China at the height of its power and spiritual inspiration when this great land was known to the world as the Middle Kingdom.

•

The driver climbed carefully down from the cab. He kept one hand on the truck's door and stood for a minute steadying himself. He bowed his aching head and closed his throbbing eyes to allow the vertigo wave to wash over him and run its course. Bile choked his throat. He knew that this would usually pass quickly but then again, what did it matter? He did have some concern about how sickly he might appear to others and thereby draw undue attention to himself. So he stood by the cab and waited for his system to adjust. As the dizziness subsided, he reached up and put both hands against the door to stretch his tired and cramped leg and back muscles. He tried a small squatting motion but immediately had to pull himself back up. His face flushed white and his legs trembled with the effort. God! He had to pull himself together; this could not happen now!

A traffic snarl had put him slightly behind schedule and this had worried and stressed him to no end. But he was now at the appointed place so he should relax. He looked down and pulled his jacket sleeve back to check his watch. It was six forty; pull yourself together! There was still twenty more minutes. He still had time.

•

The Chairman checked his watch again. He knew at that very moment special trucks were in every major city of the world. New York, Toronto, Dallas, Los Angeles, Sydney, Tokyo, Hanoi, New Delhi, Tehran, Istanbul, Berlin, Paris, London; and with each truck a lone driver, waiting and watching the time.

Tomorrow the world would awake, or what was left of it would awake to a new world controlled and ruled by the Chinese. He stood and bowed deeply and reverently to the landscape, the White Crane and to the glory of the people of the Middle Kingdom.

•

"Youse ok Mac?"

The driver turned quickly, surprised.

A large blocky and heavily bundled man was staring at him. He carried an electronic clipboard in one big-gloved hand and gestured aggressively with the other.

"Youse ok, Mac? Youse ok?"

"Yes thank you. Just a cold I think, I should be fine in a moment."

The big man took a step closer intently inspecting the driver, distrust stamped on his face.

He waved his big arm at the driver and the truck.

"Youse haven't been around any dead Africans lately have ya? I don't want no fookin E-bama death disease here on my dock, Mac!"

"No I have not encountered any Africans, dead or otherwise."

The big man stepped back.

"Asians, Africans! What's da friggin difference, Mac?"

He squinted and looked hard at the driver.

"Youse talk funny, Mac, an youse look like one fookin sick Asian to me. Youse sure you ain't got none-ah da friggin E-bama death shit, Mac?"

This was not good. It would not be prudent for this man to become too inquisitive and start questioning the contents of the trailer. There was not much time left. He put his hand into his right coat pocket and touched the control mechanism for comfort. He had a gun if need be but he had left it hidden up there in the rig. He hoped that he would not have cause to try and get to it or to use it.

"Yes thank you for your concern but it is just a cold, just a cold."

He tried to change the subject.

"I saw many birds yesterday overhead in the sky on my way here. Would you happen to know which species migrate across this land, this time of year?"

The big man eyed him distrustfully. The hairs on the back of his neck were tingling with rising anger. *This banana must be some kinda fooken tree huggin liberal fruit Chink ass-hole from commie California ur some other liberal friggin god forsaken atheist place.*

"Do ya know, Mac," he said, "what the hell is our fookin government doing letting friggin disease carrying un-Christian bastards, friggin Mexicans, fookin Chinks an Russian commie atheists an' turban wearing fake Indian Islamic terrorist in ta dis country anyway? Dat fookin president piece of shit do nuthin socialist fooken African a-hole, know that? He's bringing in every friggin diseased piece ah shit walk-en. Soon, real soon god-damn it, there won't be no more real friggin Americans left. We'd all be speak-in fooken Chink or friggin Mex-Ah-frakan Wet-Back or some fooken god-damn terro-babble shit. Know that?"

"You have an interesting accent. Where is it that you are from if I am not being too inquisitive?"

"New Jersey, Mac, so what's it too ya? Now let's move it! We can't be stand-in here shoot-in da shit all day." He looked down and checked his watch. "Time is money, Mac. This truck ain't gonna unload it friggin god-damn self."

The big man walked back around the truck to the loading dock giving the driver a wide berth. The driver watched him walk away, took a deep breath and slowly exhaled. He wondered if the big man had a wife and children. He frowned as he knew their rapidly approaching fate. It was a terrible thing to know such things.

He looked up again at the still-dark sky. A shooting pain made him close his eyes and grit his teeth. He straightened up and started off, slowly and stiffly towards the dock. He looked down to check his watch. Six more minutes, just enough time to make it up the stairs to the hopefully warm loading dock.

Warmth and family. Funny the thought that occupies one's mind in moments like this. He walked stiffly up the stairs to the dock and stood by his truck's trailer doors. He clutched the triggering device tightly in his right hand jammed deeply into his coat pocket. He surveyed the busy human and mechanical activity of the loading dock. It was visual chaos and yet upon closer inspection you could see work was accomplished with an insect like precision. No one was yet paying any attention to him. Just another worker in the collective hive.

His thoughts moved fondly to his family. Proud and yet worried about the future world his family and people would inherit. His wife and children would eventually know of the sacrifice of this group. They were assured that there would be a national monument. Streets and plazas would be named in their honor and their families promised a pension for life, but... He saw the peaceful faces of his children safe in their beds as he stood and watched them sleep, the worried eyes of his wife's beautiful face as he left their house for the last time. By tomorrow the world and its future would belong to them. He and the others were expendable, the sharp point of the great sword.

•

The Chairman sat and looked at his watch. It was time. He knew with this act that he would eclipse Stalin, Hitler, Mao, Genghis Khan, Attila and Julius Caesar as the greatest genocidal mass murder in human history. This terrible burden was his and his alone. He drank deeply from the landscape and thought of his wife and children. What would they think of what he had done? Would they despise him? Be sickened by his face and his name? Or would they understand him and this deed and why it must be done?

He thought of the people, their great country, its legacy and their future on this planet. History, it was said was written by the winners. With this act and from this day forth the history of this world would be written by his people.

•

The driver swayed and stumbled back against the trailer doors. He swallowed hard, his eyes clouding with the pain. He knew that this planet and its people would never be the same. Most would never survive.

But looking up to the birds and the beauty of the first light of the early morning sky, he knew that despite the insanity of man, nature endures. Nature always endures.

The driver smiled and with that slim hope closed his hand crushing the triggering device in his pocket. The trailer's roof blew off. Air cannons concealed inside began firing the truck's toxic cargo of highly contagious lethal airborne pathogens into the atmosphere over Washington D.C. and into the air streams that blanket the East Coast.

The driver crushed the cyanide capsule between his back teeth then repeated the words of Professor J. Robert Oppenheimer had quoted from the Bhagavad-Gita upon seeing the world's first atomic bomb blast. "Now I am become death, the destroyer of worlds."

It was twelve-noon Greenwich Mean Time the first day of the Chinese New Year.

Revere the Rain

By Lisa Meltzer Penn

The California sun, our Marilyn Monroe of weather
has called for a break
a little privacy for a change
cover of gray

A week of rain, a steady beat
No flux, no false promise
My weather app displays five miniature boxes of
        raindrops
And produces another box each day

I drive through the rain to the gym
go upstairs and into the vise-like grip of the abductor
My thigh muscles push out
flex back, push out again

A flat, brittle field below puddles the rain
while a flock of geese roves through the newly sprung
        weeds
feather edges growing misty
as they pull the greening up and out of the ground

Through the window I watch as the outside layer of
        gray
grows softer and more indistinct
the ramparts blurring
the weight room inside a dream of a dream

The abductor machine is set up to face its foster twin—
    the adductor
Metal plates pressed in forced companionship, a thing
    and its reflection
I point at the windows
"Did you see?" I blurt out to the woman facing me

"I know!" she says, blowing a wisp of hair off her face
"It's despicable, isn't it?"
"No, it's *beautiful*," I insist
"Huh," she says. "I thought I left all that behind."

It turns out we share wet and muddy east coast roots,
    different towns
Maybe that's why our knees and voices almost but
    don't quite touch
We finish our repetitions and switch places
Now she faces the window and I am her reflection.

With a final set, I bequeath to her my wishes
Push in: rain. Back out: soft gray
Push in: possibility. Back out: magic
I smile a little and head down the stairs

Outside, of course, it is wetter than it looked from
    above
Not just floating mist
I unhinge my soggy umbrella
The spring pops up violently

The gangly geese don't look up from their smorgasbord
Their winged and waterproof bodies made for this day
Tail feathers point to the sky
Beaks jab in and out of the earth

Like the geese and the softening ground, I adore and
      revere the rain
A breathy echo of Marilyn calls, *"A smart girl leaves*
      before she is left."
At that moment my sneakers and umbrella lose the
      last
of their imperviousness and the rain soaks through.

The Dream-Walk-While-Awake
By Marjorie Bicknell Johnson

Where was this jade found? Chanla Pesh, fondling her shaman's talisman and lost in thought, sat at her desk in the bedroom of her quiet apartment in Austin, Texas. As a lecturer in Mayan Studies at the university, she had told no one that she was a shaman. She stared at the reclining jaguar carved from jade, dark chatoyant green, its luster changing like a cat's eye, and became more curious by the minute. While the Maya had told no one where they found jade, she could find the history of her jade jaguar through a dream-walk.

In a vision years ago, she had merged with King Itzamná B'alam and watched his scribes paint glyphs in vibrant red, green, and blue onto whitewashed pages. They stored the finished book in an elaborately carved wooden box, and the king hid it from the Spaniards. She found the box and the book in a hollow temple step where he had hidden it at the B'alam Witz ruin.

As an archaeologist, she found being a shaman had advantages. Through visions, she could visit ancient buildings, the better to sketch them; she could follow long-dead persons, the better to read ancient script; and she could track down looters, the better to recover stolen artifacts.

Her talisman had been found in a cave behind that very ruin. By ancient custom, the Maya would have placed it there in the grave of a king. She could look for it again, but she had failed once before. She needed a deeper trance, the *dream-walk-while-awake*.

To enter such a state, her grandmother Chiich had sprinkled three drops of her own royal blood, a pinch of dream-mushroom, and a crumble of *copal* incense over a fire. Her visions came when she breathed the sweet-smelling smoke.

Pesh didn't need all that to induce a guided daydream for a vision journey, but to trace the talisman, she had to fall into a deep trance. Her students had given her a lump of incense in a candle cup. She lit it and waited for its pungent smoke. Holding her obsidian ritual bloodletting knife, the blade so sharp it could sever a finger without pain, she nicked her left thumb. Three drops of royal blood fell onto the jade jaguar's back. She sat cross-legged on the bedroom's hardwood floor and inhaled incense smoke.

To fix her concentration, Pesh rubbed the smooth head of her jade jaguar and closed her eyes to let pictures form on the inside of her eyelids. She fingered blades of grass toughened by the dry climate. Sunlight filtered through tree leaves and vines, and leaf ants crossed the trail in single file. She channeled the screams of howler monkeys, the smell of vanilla orchids, the feel of a fly on her nose, to a day in the jungle. She forced stray thoughts and chatter out of her mind until she was there, at B'alam Witz, sometime in the past.

The jungle then had the same heavy air, the same sweet smell. *Chanlajun Pex Yaxuun B'alam*, her Maya self, rested hidden beneath a tree at dusk. Crickets sang in the symphony of the forest and beetles buzzed in rhythm. She crushed grass-that-smells-like-lemon on her skin to repel insects and stretched the muscles in her arms and legs.

Then, a Maya man materialized and her spirit slipped into his body. She rubbed oil on her face—it was his face, his handsome face, his forehead flat and sloping back in the classic style. He rubbed the hard muscles in his chest, stretched his arms, and ran his fingers through his hair. She saw the moon and the white road through his eyes and smelled orchids through his nose and breathed through his mouth. She had meshed with the Maya warrior *Sac B'alam Ahau*, the white jaguar lord.

The kings and princes at B'alam Witz had taken the name *B'alam* for untold generations. Sac B'alam held the jade jaguar in his right hand and felt its smoothness. He moved the talisman across his chest in the sign of the Mayan cross—right to left as the sun moves from east to west and up and down from the heavens to the earth. He asked B'alam, the jaguar god of the underworld and patron god of war, to bless the amulet. Afterward, he placed it in his deerskin bag.

Illuminated by the moon, Sac B'alam loped along a *sacbé,* a white plastered road connecting northern Mayan cities. He had to bring the jade jaguar to his twin brother to put on their grandfather's grave, as was the custom.

The scene shifted. Sac B'alam, his brother Pakal, and four Maya warriors entered the caves. They held pitch torches and plodded down, deep into the dark, and turned to the right. Sac B'alam led them in prayer to the gods of the underworld and placed the jaguar talisman beside the grandfather, a mummy wrapped in blue woven cloth.

Pakal reminded his brother that, on their return, he had to smash the path behind them so the spirits would remain in *Xibalba*, land of the dead.

After the first swing of his jade sledgehammer, Sac B'alam shed Pesh as though she were the skin of a snake. Separated from Sac B'alam, she drifted between worlds. The men left her there, in the dark cave—the sacred cave where she would become a shaman in a few centuries. The scene went black. She couldn't bring it back.

"Hear me, O gods of *Xibalba*! Which way?" she cried out in Mayan.

"You—again? Needing our help to leave the cave? Ha-ha-ha!" The voice boomed out of the dark, behind her, all around her. "Why call on us?"

Pesh cringed. *Cimil*, evil god of the underworld!

"You have forsaken us for years," he bellowed. "You are a fallen *Xmenoob*."

Pesh did not answer. Cold swept up her legs and through her buttocks and spread to her shoulders and the top of her neck. She could not move. She had ventured too close to *Xibalba*, the underworld land of spirits with no time. *Xibalba*: where the gods had claimed her as a shaman and given her the special powers of *Xmenoob*.

Forsaken for years— Did Cimil know that she had taken her baby Yash to be christened in the Catholic Church? Was that it? She had asked for wedding blessings from *Hun Hunahpu,* god of the corn harvest, at the temple at B'alam Witz, but that was before Yash but far in the future.

"Only the gods know where jade comes from," Cimil thundered.

"Find the lost jade, your salvation," said a second voice, less threatening. "A wager: you win when you find the lost jade."

The Trickster? What lost jade? Was that a riddle? She trembled.

"Find where your talisman comes from," a third god roared. "Without our help."

Pesh groaned and put her hands over her ears.

"We will tell you where the jade jaguar came from," Cimil said, his voice an unpleasant cackle, "but your first-born daughter will become a shaman."

The cave turned black. The torches were gone, not even the glow of an ember. The heavy blackness pushed her down, down to death.

"No! Never!" Screaming, Pesh emerged from the vision, her heart pounding. Sweat poured down her face. She lay in a heap on the bedroom floor, her muscles jerking. She felt like an arrow had skewered her skull, the sharp and insistent pain made worse by sunlight streaming through the window.

After the twitching stopped, she sat up, nauseated and unsteady. The room spun.

What was in that incense? She held her head in her hands and swallowed bile.

Grandmother Chiich had warned her, if a shaman—especially one of the chosen ones—did not fulfill the duties given by the gods, she would suffer. Pesh suffered now, as if a knife twisted in her stomach, joining the barbed blade in her head. She steadied herself against a chair.

Yes, she was one of the *Xmenoob*, a shaman by blood, as Chiich had been before her. A fallen *Xmenoob*— What did that mean? Even though she no longer practiced the old religion, she always wore her jaguar talisman next to her skin. The lucky totem given to her by the gods in the sacred cave: she felt it now for comfort.

Pesh took out Chiich's small linen satchel, hidden at the back of her dresser, and fingered its sacred pebbles. Jade, the green of life and the earth; amber, yellow for the compass point south; cinnabar, red for east; quartz, white for north; and obsidian, black for west: the colors of the Cosmos.

Each stone, like every word in Mayan, had several meanings. The Mayan word *ya'ax* was used either for blue or for green, the colors found in the sacred quetzal's tail. Her ancestral name *Yaxuun B'alam* meant "precious-bird jaguar" or the king who had given her his DNA. And *yax* meant precious, sacred, or even jade. Would anything be different, if she knew how to use the stones?

A fallen *Xmenoob*: a disgraced shaman. Her shoulders heaved with dry sobs that became shivers. She rubbed her throbbing stomach, rocked back and forth, grieved for her loss, as though an obsidian knife had stolen a fetus. She felt the fetus kicking, a phantom fetus, like an amputee with an aching phantom limb. Even her jade talisman gave her no comfort.

She shook her head. She was an American citizen, a lecturer at the university. She could tell no one about her encounter with Cimil—hearing voices from unfamiliar gods from a thousand years ago. But she couldn't live like this, in periodic states of anxiety. Cimil had hurled a challenge, like a jade spear lodged in her skull.

She held the jade talisman and watched sunlight shimmer down the jaguar's back from its head to its tail. A man, not a god, had placed it in the cave. A man, not a god, had carved it. A man, not a god, had found the raw stone.

She would find the lost jade, herself. With no help from the gods. She would journey from Austin to B'alam Witz to wherever the talisman was carved, to wherever it had begun.

meditation

By Maurine Killough

this is the way life is with its boxes and swirls
appearing as snares, suction cups and mazes
they are everywhere
you step into them every day, get boxed in
circle around and around then trip into a dead end
before you see clearly, after so many lifetimes
that the boxes are windows
the swirls are clouds to carry you away
the rubik's cubes are your own lethal thoughts
so i lie down to not think
i am awake but i do not participate
i recline quietly as ancient labyrinths order my
    hair
secret mazes mark my body
sacred swirls coil my mind
cyclones siphon my drops
i shut my drain pipes to all that is going on
like music in the background and fall into myself
into my infinity
spiral like a snake where gaia meets the cosmos
let the energy flow
fly above where the patterns take helix shape
until i am free of the circling thoughts, material
    traps
and can wrap my being around
the divine pattern
of all that there is

Going Revolutionary

By Laurel Anne Hill

I dashed out of the Tumbleweed Community Center, one hand clutching my cell phone and the other wrapped around an open can of Pepsi. The wall of Mojave heat hit me. My backpack practically melted against my blouse. I didn't need this hot air from Hell. I had a dead-celebrity show going on. The great Enrico Caruso had crossed over from the other side to entertain his fans—and brought bad luck with him. I needed to find Great-Grandpa's ghost. Fast.

My eyes scanned the crowded parking lot. No sign of Great-Grandpa Villa. Well, he sure wasn't inside. I'd signaled his spirit frequency for five minutes straight. I should have upgraded my host-a-ghost app. Hell, I should have done a lot of things. Maybe then I would've landed a contract to host Elvis, who still refused to visit the land of the living.

Ethereal gray tufts—like the spirits of scattered cotton balls—headed in my direction. Great-Grandpa, thank God. His unattached little finger collided with my shoulder. His eyeball bounced off his gaudy pinky ring. He'd duplicated Elvis' lion ring last November. To celebrate the anniversary of Elvis' movie, *Fun in Acapulco*, or so he claimed. More likely he'd done it to show he could.

"We've a problem," I said, "have to leave soon." For some reason I smelled licorice. "Where've you been?"

"My pieces." His lion ring's diamond eyes flashed in my direction. "They like talking with my fans."

I groaned. Grave robbers had dug up his corpse years ago and stolen his head. His trigger finger had ended up in an El Paso pawnshop. How gross and embarrassing, the way he kept self-dismembering and reassembling his ghost for a publicity stunt. Sometimes I wished Great-Grandpa wasn't Pancho Villa, the famous Mexican revolutionary.

"The hole." I shoved my cell phone into the pocket of my white jeans. "The one in the wall of the eternity continuum you and Caruso used." Had that only been four days ago? "It's closing. The hydrogen sulfide readings there are dropping fast. We've got until two o'clock at the latest to get Caruso back. I'm cutting his program short."

"*Tierra y libertad*. Land and Liberty." Great-Grandpa's boxy, translucent head—minus his eyeballs—grinned. "The time to revolt for Mexico draws near."

Crap! Caruso's existence and my host-a-ghost venture teetered on the precipice of disaster. My bank account wilted from a starvation diet. And Great-Grandpa was going revolutionary again.

"Forget battle cries," I said. The Mexican Revolution had happened a century ago. Why would I, a hundred-pound weakling and U.S. citizen, ever jump into a fight for Mexico? "Focus on our real problem."

"Sometimes I think," Great-Grandpa said, "you and me, Alyssa, we no related."

God, I'd disappointed him again. He always did the broken English thing with me when he got frustrated. But most spirits weren't as hardy as he was. Caruso would likely disintegrate if he hung around this world for long. Not Great-Grandpa, though. Pancho Villa had defined his own rules in life and did likewise in death. What other spook could mess around with their shape so well?

"Gather yourself. Please." I gulped down the rest of my Pepsi, set the empty in a planter box, then pulled my special sack out of my backpack. "I need to fetch Caruso."

His ethereal head nodded. His mustache drooped. A stream of his body parts rolled toward the waiting sack. His torso, cross-strapped with two bandoliers full of bullets, shrank to a spindle of smoke before entering.

"Alyssa," Great-Grandpa said. "I no talk about a guns-and-bullets Mexican revolt. I talk about doing something revolutionary for Mexicans."

No guns? That was good.

"King Elvis who'll live forever will help us," he added. "Wait and see."

King Elvis. Ever since Great-Grandpa's spirit had come to me several years ago with his ghost-hosting scheme to get me out of debt, he'd promised to bring me Elvis. But then, he'd once promised Great-Grandma he'd marry her. Never had. At least no other ghost-hosts had snagged the King. Not yet.

•

The community center had a boxy design style best described as modern cheap. About three hundred attendees jammed the main assembly room. No wonder the air-conditioning system struggled.

Once again, I scanned the audience for potential troublemakers. Nobody shifted their gaze around the room, looking like they'd traveled to the Emerald City of Oz to tear down the wizard's curtain. Zero skeptics. Maybe because the world's Caruso impersonators—living or dead—probably totaled less than ten. Elvis impersonators, however, would be a different matter. If the time ever came, could I convince people I promoted the real thing?

A thin, hollow voice drifted in my direction—Enrico Caruso, or what was left of him. The late, famous tenor reminisced about the 1906 earthquake in San Francisco. This particular story would end soon. I checked the time.

"Alyssa," Great-Grandpa said from inside the bag. "What did you do with your empty Pepsi can?"

"Shhh," I said. Why did he care where I'd put a soft drink container? "Let Caruso finish."

"Then we ran down the stairs and into the street," Caruso rasped.

Caruso's ethereal face flickered like a flame in a draft. The cleft in his chin. The slight upturn of his closed-mouth smile. His translucent figure, dressed in a tuxedo, shimmered multiple hues of turquoise, blue and gray.

Unfortunately, he'd not sing in public this afternoon. Or ever again. In 1921, his legendary voice had succumbed with his body. Hadn't seemed to affect ticket sales. Opera lovers adored Caruso's mystique.

Had death destroyed Elvis's voice? If so, he might fear a negative reaction from his fans. Was that why The King hadn't crossed over yet?

Well, if I ever managed to book Elvis, I'd need immediate access to a huge facility. Not in Mexico. Elvis's derogatory remarks about Mexicans once started a riot there. How could Great-Grandpa think the ghost of Elvis would even trust him, let alone do something revolutionary to help Mexicans? Maybe he wanted some sort of a benefit concert for needy Mexican immigrants. Elvis might buy into that.

Church bells chimed in the distance. Twelve noon arrived. Caruso's time in this world, once again, was up.

"Conclusions please, Mr. Caruso," I asserted.

He would know my meaning. The audience would, too.

"I got no lion ring," Great-Grandpa mumbled.

"What are you talking about?"

"I think it's in the empty Pepsi can," he said.

How the hell had any part of Great-Grandpa ended up there? I so did not need this.

•

My ancient pickup truck bumped along the unpaved road through the blistering heat, Caruso, Great-Grandpa and the Pepsi can inside my sack. Twelve-fifty-five. The eternity rift could close earlier than I'd calculated. Would I get there in time?

My signal receiver beeped like car horns in a traffic jam. GPS coordinates claimed I neared the transmitter and fake boulder I'd planted in plain sight four days ago. I slowed my pickup and scanned the flat, barren ground.

I drew in a deep breath. No rotten egg odor. Had the fissure finished closing? A tumbleweed rolled across my path. The wind didn't blow directly toward me. The next gust carried a faint smell of sulfides. I prayed I'd arrived in time.

Up ahead, my rock waited, two feet long, wide and high. I braked the pickup, then climbed out. The rift lay somewhere above that camouflaged chunk of concrete. What opening remained and how far up, I couldn't tell. The ghosts would have to find the portal before it glued itself shut. Who knew when or where the next gateway would appear?

"I can't detect the fissure." I opened the spook sack. "Hurry up."

Great-Grandpa swirled out of the bag. At least he was together in one piece. No, his pinky and lion ring were missing.

"This is all me," he said, with a dismissive wave of his hand. "I redistributed for revolution."

Not the first time he'd practically read my mind. Explanations would have to wait.

He led Caruso upward in the air, forming a thin twisting column of spirit smoke. Twenty feet above me. Higher. The wind neither shifted nor dispersed them. My tongue tasted metal. The spirits sparkled all silvery. The sun shone through them, transmuting silver into gold—ghostly alchemy. The ghosts and metallic flavor vanished.

A release of inner tension sagged my shoulders. Caruso was safe. I hadn't killed a ghost. It was time to get going. I'd retrieve my rock later. I removed the Pepsi can from my spook sack and smelled licorice. Where did that odor keep coming from? I tossed the sack into my pickup, then stepped backward and stood up straight. My scalp prickled, my shoulder-length brown hair a plaything of the rising wind.

My dad had used Brut aftershave. It had smelled faintly of licorice. I hadn't thought of him shaving for years.

"Oh, my God," I whispered.

Elvis had used Brut, too, hadn't he? And Elvis had loved...to drink Pepsi.

What if Great-Grandpa's lion ring hadn't ever been part of him? What if it was all of Elvis? Great-Grandpa might have taught him how to alter shape. But that would mean Elvis had been crossing over with Great-Grandpa since last November. He should have disintegrated.

Or was he vulnerable in that way? Great-Grandpa had referred to King Elvis, who would live forever.

I sat on the ground. My index finger traced the Pepsi-Cola trademark on the aluminum can in my grasp. The King in my care. Millions of dollars. Could it be true? I tipped the can.

"Hello," I said. "Anybody home in there?"

A scorching wind arose, blasting me from behind like the proverbial one from Hell. Still holding the Pepsi can, I jumped to my feet. I crossed my arms against my chest, my eyes wide. My stomach felt like a piece of line in a knot-tying class.

"Land and liberty," Great-Grandpa said. "I did what you wanted. Your turn now."

How could I hear him? I'd seen him spiral toward the rift. All of him had returned to the other side of the eternity continuum.

Wait a minute. Great-Grandpa had redistributed and claimed his ghost was all him. Not that his ghost was all OF him. His pinky had been missing.

"My people," Great-Grandpa said, "deserve the right to trod upon land they once owned."

The voice came from the inside of my head. He'd fucking lodged a piece of himself in my ear.

"Miss Alyssa." His voice echoed. "Tear down this wall."

Wall? What wall? What did he—

Oh, my God, *THE WALL*. He'd meant the one along the U.S. Mexican Border.

I could imagine it. Elvis on the wall's Mexican side, signing autographs. Border agents leaving their posts to get one. Twitter going insane. Millions of Elvis fans gathering at the wall's U.S. side. Members of Congress inundated with emails from constituents. My jaws and stomach clenched.

Great-Grandpa wanted me to instigate an international incident. Trigger a revolution in U.S. immigration policies. Probably get tossed into jail. That sucked!

"You still there, Miss Alyssa?" a deep, resonant voice said. A love-me-tender, peace-in-the-valley, unmistakable Elvis croon came from inside the Pepsi can.

"Yes." My voice squeaked.

Obviously, Elvis couldn't hear what Great-Grandpa said inside my ear. At least death hadn't diminished The King's magnificent voice.

"I'm Johnny Cash. Just kiddin'." Elvis made a deep, guttural noise, as if clearing his throat. "Mr. Villa must have been hot on land and liberty. He sure whooped a lot of asses to get 'em."

"Yeah, he did."

Elvis used to use a Johnny Cash introductory line on stage for an ice-breaker. Being here on his own must have triggered his anxiety. My nerves could beat his nerves.

"I'm Pancho Villa," I said to Elvis. "Part of me, anyway. And I don't think I'm kidding."

"Swear to God?" A curl of spirit smoke drifted up from the Pepsi can. "Well, I sure like your Great-Grandpa, Miss Pancho-Alyssa. And I like how you care about the safety of your ghost guests. Where you goin' ta book me first? Graceland, Los Angeles or New York City?"

"Over my dead body," the wisp of Great-Grandpa shouted inside my ear.

A play on words? Or the closest thing to a threat he'd ever spewed in my direction? My stomach did a back flip. In life, Pancho Villa had been a bandit as well as a hero. He hadn't treated traitors with compassion.

Well, Great-Grandpa might stop bringing me ghosts to host, but Great-Grandma wouldn't let him harm me in any physical way. Still, during the Mexican revolution, they'd fought to improve the living conditions and dignity of the Mexican underclass. The only thing I ever fought for was a healthy bank account. What did they really think of me? I pressed my dry lips together.

"I loved your movie, *Fun in Acapulco*," I said to Elvis. "While I make arrangements for your U.S. tour, you ought to build up your fan base in Mexico." Was I really saying this? "We'll create a flash mob spectacular along the U.S./Mexican border."

Tierra y libertad. Hell, I was Pancho Villa's great-granddaughter, wasn't I? How gross to keep embarrassing him.

We had a show to put on.

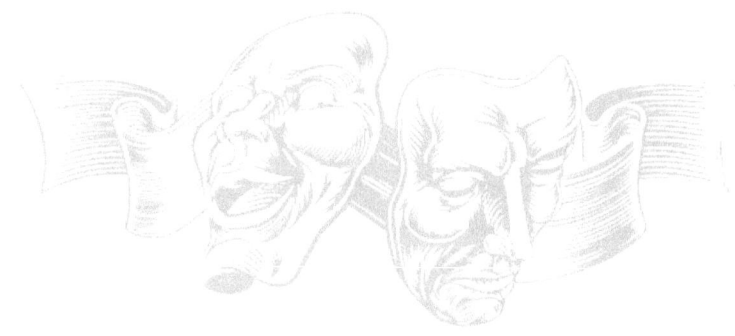

Movie

Jim Stanfield

Circled by a thousand Hollywooden Indians
our pioneering pilgrim's trek begins
He plods past lengthy shadows done
by rocks and unrelenting sun
For whose amusement was this battle staged
fearless forces for the ages raged
Who am I kidding, only me
whether a featured player or an extra be
Usurping nature's ageless monument
for some feeble writer's cemetery plot
Boot hill, the obligatory, inescapable cliché
To indicate a change of place or time of day
the educated editor inserts a lap dissolve
On just such tricks does continuity revolve
The stones of wood, the iron gate
A few choice words to stay my fate
I cleared the cobwebs from the lock
to leave my mark upon the rock
Not quite anachronism free, I fly
contrails across a cowboy movie sky
Which, through the framing lens he spied
cut, the dour director cried

Author Bios

Kevin Arnold is a writer from Portola Valley, California. These are his second and third stories in *Fault Zone* this year, a year he's also been published in *Slippery Elm; Fresh Hot Bread; Wine, Cheese, and Chocolate;* and has a poem forthcoming in the *Willow Glen Poetry Project* anthology and *Mudfish*. Based on a story extracted from one of his novels, the San Francisco /Peninsula California Writer's Club named him Writer of the Year, 2014-2015.

Sue Barizon, the daughter of immigrant parents, was born in San Francisco and raised in San Mateo. She writes mostly memoir about life's lessons learned growing up in mid-century suburbia. She began writing as a means to "quiet the buzzing in my head left by the Jiminy Cricket moments of my youth." Two of her short stories, "The Garbageman's Daughter" and "Off Guard" have been published in *Fault Zone* anthologies. She was awarded 2013 Writer of the Year Award by the San Francisco/Peninsula Writers, a branch of the California Writers Club. She serves as assistant director for the San Mateo County Fair Literary Arts Stage.

Bill Baynes is a writer, producer and director. He has been a reporter for the Miami Herald and the Associated Press and won awards as a documentary filmmaker. He has been active in feature film and video production, magazine publishing, public interest marketing and website development. He has worked with school systems to create student-driven media campaigns about health-related topics. His novel *Bunt!* was published by Silverback Sages, New Mexico. He is a member of the board of the California Writers Club, Peninsula Branch.

Jo Carpignano writes poetry, memoirs, short stories and travel adventures, many of which have been published in anthologies and national magazines. Her poetry has won several awards. In 2013 her poem "Elegy to a Beloved

Colleague" earned her title of National Senior Poet Laureate; and in 2011, the poem, "Yellow Bus" won the California Senior Poet Laureate award. Jo has also published a biography of her mother's immigrant experience, entitled *Madeline's Story*. A retired educator and school psychologist, Jo lives in San Mateo, California.

Belinda Chua has a background in healthcare and is new to writing. She is interested in personal essays and short fiction.

Ann Foster was the 2011 recipient of the Jack London Award of the SF/Peninsula Writers, a branch of the California Writers Club, and winner of the 2011 Foster City Writing Contest, personal essay division. She has served as treasurer and membership chair of the branch, and currently serves as reservations chair. Ann writes fiction and narrative nonfiction, and her work is published in *Fault Zone*, and *The Sand Hill Review*. She is now working on a novel set in post-Civil War Missouri and Texas.

Darlene Frank is a writer, editor, and creativity coach who helps people navigate their writing journey and produce powerful work. She especially enjoys working with people who have undergone a radical life transformation and want to create art from that experience. Her creative nonfiction (mostly memoir) appears in several anthologies, including the last five issues of *Fault Zone*. www.darlenefrankwriting.com

Jeannine Gerkman is a person with many hats—Poet, Realtor, Volunteer, Fashion Consultant, Artist, Dog Mom. She has written over 60 poems, some of them prize-winning and published. A Realtor since 1997, she delights in helping folks market and sell their homes in the Bay Area, focusing on Belmont.

Laurel Anne Hill's award-winning novel, *Heroes Arise,* was published by KOMENAR in 2007. Her many short stories and nonfiction pieces have appeared in a variety of publications, most recently in the anthologies *Horror Addicts Guide to Life*, *A Bard Day's Knight*, *Fault Zone*, and *Shanghai Steam*. *Shanghai Steam*, nominated for an Aurora Award in 2013, is recommended by *Writing Fantasy & Science Fiction*. Please note that Laurel wrote her short story, "Going Revolutionary," in honor of her Mexican great-grandfather. He triggered an international incident between Mexico and the United States in 1886. More at www.laurelannehill.com.

Diane Jacobson, a true Montana girl, is weathering the Bay Area with her Pandora app tuned to country music, an arsenal of fish stories at the ready, a Leatherman tool in her purse, and a row of boots in her closet. She lives in San Carlos with her husband, son, and two dogs where she is at work on short fiction and novels. "Love Doctor" is excerpted from a novel in progress.

Michele Jessen's award-winning poetry has been published in three volumes of *Carry the Light*. She is a member of the San Francisco/Peninsula Branch of California Writers Club and lives and works on the Peninsula.

Marjorie Bicknell Johnson started writing fiction in 2002; prior to that, she wrote many mathematical articles that have appeared in various academic journals. She has two published novels, *Bird Watcher* and *Jaguar Princess,* and her prize-winning short stories are published in anthologies. Currently, she is the managing editor of *WritersTalk*, the newsletter from South Bay Writers. Marjorie also is a pilot and a mathematician specializing in Fibonacci numbers.

Beverly Kalinin has published three books on transformation: *Supermom Wonderwife: Tales of Transition*, women's poetry, Morningsun Publications; *Power to the Dancers!,* creative nonfiction, Metamorphous Press; and, most recently, *Alone on the Yellow Brick Road*, memoir, Robertson Publishing. In addition, she has written a picture-book series, *The Serra Series*; a stage play,

Mandala; and a novel, *Let the Fire Fall*. Her newspaper and magazine articles, along with her poetry and children's stories, have appeared in local and national publications.

Sam Kauffman, an internationally known Christian author, poet, singer, songwriter, workshop presenter, dramatist and recording artist, is a published musician and poet. Born in Seattle, WA, Sam majored in music and English at the University of Washington. Now living in the San Francisco Bay Area, Sam travels nationally and internationally performing concerts, one woman dramas, specialty programs and workshops on storytelling and drama, along with adjudicating national vocal competitions. She has been an Author in Residence.

Maurine Killough is a two-time first place winner for free-form poetry at the San Mateo County Fair and is a regular feature at Bay Area readings. She has been published by Tayen Lane Publishing, Sandhill Press and a scattering of online and small press publications. Visit her poetry blog which features the art of local artists matched with poems at iwritemyself.wordpress.com

Ida J. Lewenstein is a retired English-as-a-Second-Language instructor of some twenty-two years and wears several hats. She has written poems, chants, and rhymes to reinforce the structures she was teaching in a fun way. Some of these have worked their way into imaginative story poems for children. She is an active member of the California Writers Club, and some of her poems have been published in *Fault Zone: Words for the Edge*, *Fault Zone: Stepping up to the Edge*, and now *Fault Zone: Transform*.

Diane Lee Moomey has lived and wandered around the US and Canada, and now dips her gardener's hands in California dirt. A regular reader at Willow Glen Poetry, Florey's in Pacifica, and other Bay Area venues, she has published prose and poetry, most recently in the *Sand Hill Review* and *Red Wheelbarrow*, and has been nominated for a Pushcart prize. She has also published three books under her own imprint, DaysEye Press and Studios. To read more, please visit www.pw.org/content/diane_moomey. Diane is also a watercolorist and collage artist, an experience that both seeds and is seeded by, her poetic imagery. To view her artwork, please visit www.dianeleemoomeyart.com

Lisa Meltzer Penn has contributed short stories, prose poetry, and novel excerpts to multiple *Fault Zone* anthologies. Her work also appears in the *Sand Hill Review XII*; *Best of the Sand Hill Review*; *Travelers Tales: Spain*; *Travelers Tales: San Francisco*; *Transfer Magazine* and *The Cupboard*. With an extensive background in New York publishing, Lisa has worked hands-on with authors on both coasts for thirty years, and served as founding editor of the *Fault Zone* series. She now lives with her husband, two children, and dog on the Peninsula.

TR Poulson, a University of Nevada, Reno alum, lives in East Palo Alto, California. Her work has appeared in *Alehouse, Trajectory, The Meadow, Verdad, Raintown Review*, and *J Journal*. She enjoys quality time spent with her nieces and nephew, as well as windsurfing, zumba, basketball, and horse racing. "Sweet Harmony" is a celebration of the sport that she loves: the beauty, the tragedies, and the power we have to overcome hardship.

Don Redman has been published in a previous Fault Zone, and various automotive racing and classic car magazines. He has received international awards for the latter and has all of his original teeth.

Frank A. Saunders writes poetry, fiction, scientific articles, and music, most recently the portfolio *A Scent of Tea*. He lives in Foster City with his wife, Barbara, and daughter, Andrea. He has taught physiological psychology at San Francisco State University and is a licensed clinical neuropsychologist. Visit his website at www.frankasaunders.com.

Martha Clark Scala has a split personality as a writer and psychotherapist. Her poetry has appeared in *Porter Gulch Review, Poetry Now, Fault Zone* and *Home for the Holidays*. Martha's writing on grief-related issues can be found in *We Need Not Walk Alone* (published by The Compassionate Friends), *The California Therapist, SCV-CAMFT News, www.caring.com, California Therapist, SCV-CAMFT News*, www.caring.com, and at her website, www.mcscala.com. Martha publishes a monthly e-newsletter, "Out On a Limb" which focuses on bringing joy back to our lives.

Jim Stanfield is a retired Mechanical Designer who put in twenty-seven years at SLAC National Accelerator Lab, formerly Stanford Linear Accelerator Center, as an Associate Engineer. Jim specializes in scientific humor and has been published in the pages of "The Journal of Irreproducible Results" and the *Sand Hill Review*. Starting from the age of four, he is an avid amateur photographer. Jim is also the co-founder of The Institute for Further Research.

Dave M. Strom is a technical writer who has written about superheroine Holly Hansson since Dan Brown's book The DaVinci Code. He has read comic books since Stan Lee created Spider-Man. Dave's goals: put funny back into superhero stories, and have superheroines clobber villains without being a superhero clone: Superman/Supergirl, Batman/Batgirl, Ant-Man/Wasp, Hulk/She-Hulk, do you see a pattern? Dave likes to write, read, eat Pho, watch decent cartoons, perform at open mics, make people laugh, and find great superhero/superheroine stories on Kindle.

Ollie Mae Trost Welch has a degree in creative writing and English Literature. She is a writer of fiction, non-fiction, poems, and plays. She has written a novel and five novellas. Her memoir has been published and her poems have appeared in many venues. One of her plays was performed at Dominican University and won six awards.

Nanci Lee Woody taught school, wrote college-level math and accounting textbooks, and served as Dean of Business at American River College. Her first novel, *Tears and Trombones*, published by Sand Hill Review Press, won an IPPY (Independent Publishers Book Awards) for Best Fiction in the Western Pacific Region. Nanci has also published short stories and poetry in anthologies and online. She is a photographer and draws and paints. Her artwork has appeared in numerous juried shows in the Sacramento area and in the KVIE (PBS) annual on-air fundraising auctions. Her Amazon Author's Page is at amazon.com/author/nancileewoody.com